CHILDREN *of* ANGELS

BOOK ONE OF THE NEW NEPHILIM SERIES

KATHRYN DAHLSTROM

WinePressPublishing
Great Books, Defined.

WinePress Publishing (PO Box 428, Enumclaw, WA 98022) functions only as book publisher. As such, the ultimate design, content, editorial accuracy, and views expressed or implied in this work are those of the author.

ISBN 13: 978-1-60615-216-4
ISBN 10: 1-60615-216-5
Library of Congress Catalog Card Number: 2010938095

CONTENTS

ACKNOWLEDGMENTS

MY DEEPEST THANKS for the undying support of my husband Tim, my mom Dorothy Shetler, my daughter Kristina, my prayer friends Diane Gunion, Deb Hass, and Peggy Opheim, my friends in Screenwriting U, and my church, North Branch United Methodist.

Thanks to Producer Hal Croasmun for making me find the core of this story, and to my test reader, Emily Greene, for convincing me that kids could like it.

And all praise and thanks to the Captain of my dreams, the LORD Jesus Christ.

Chapter 1

THE DAY

I T'S THE SON of the sleaze ball!" someone yelled behind him. Jeremy Lapoint felt heat hit his face. Great. The perfect ending of another good day!

He had blond hair in a mess of tight curls, blue eyes, and fair skin that showed him blushing from a mile away. He kept walking, keeping his eyes ahead. The last leaves on the oaks lining the street stood out burgundy red in the mild sun of a November afternoon. Too bad he couldn't enjoy the nice weather while it lasted.

He recognized the shouter's voice—Sid Lundahl. His words jabbed Jeremy's back as though they were darts—not those suction cup things, either—the real ones with the steel points like Dad used to throw at the dartboard in the basement. The dartboard, the basement, and Dad were all gone now. Jeremy, his mom, and younger sister, Dana, lived in a second-floor apartment, and Dad was in prison for armed robbery.

He'd been there for four years. Jeremy would never know how Sid found out what Dad had done, but he'd swaggered down the crowded seventh grade hall of Anoka, Minnesota, Middle School on the first day, two months ago, bellowed it out loud three feet from Jeremy's locker, and enjoyed the ripple effect.

Sid had at least four followers with him at all times. They were all large for seventh graders and they knew it. Jeremy had his own name for them: the Big Butt Gang.

Before he knew what happened, Sid's best friend, Chad, clamped a pudgy hand on Jeremy's backpack—his faded, raveling Spiderman bag that his cousin in fourth grade would consider childish. Jeremy had to carry his stuff in something. Chad yanked the pack off his shoulders before his victim could spin and make a grab for the straps.

Sid caught Jeremy's shoulder and jerked him back. "Settle down. We're just curious."

Chad unzipped the main compartment and dumped Jeremy's books, folders, and papers on the ground, stomping on his science report that was due tomorrow, grinding it underfoot until it ripped. But the worst came when he opened the small outer pocket. He pulled out Jeremy's new iPod. It was his best birthday present. He'd had it less than two weeks. "That's from my grandma!"

THE DAY

Chad dropped the iPod and leaped, landing on it with both heels. *C-r-r-runch*!

"Prob'ly stolen, anyway," said Sid.

Jeremy seized the pack, still in Chad's arms, and wrenched it away from him so hard that he pulled the right strap loose at the top. He swung the bag back and forth at all five of his harassers as though it was a baseball bat. The bag pelted Sid's face. The dangling strap—now a whip—slapped Chad's shoulder and whapped a third bully on the neck. The toughs yelped in pain and scrambled to a safe distance. Sid led the retreat. "Since when do you fight back, wussy boy?"

Younger kids noticed the fray and ran two blocks away to the crossing guard, an older lady in a blaze green vest with orange bands. She loosed a shout. Sid, quick to pick up such signals, hustled his crew away at a fast walk. They kept their faces and movements cool, but he had to toss back a threat. "That hurt, loser. Payback's coming."

They broke into trots and crossed the street, disappearing around the corner.

Jeremy, groaning, gathered his mangled papers and dirt-stained books.

A cluster of seventh grade girls divided and rushed past him as if he wasn't there. Their talk and laughter was sharp to his ears until it left him behind, a reminder that he was alone, as usual.

Why did these things keep happening? Why couldn't kids like Sid leave him alone? The iPod was worth around two hundred dollars, and it didn't look fixable, nor could Mom afford to buy him another one. He'd heard her muttering over the bills last night. She didn't know how she was going to pay the rent this month.

Rage roiled up in him. He pounced on a broken brick lying by a tree and took aim at a dumpster at the far end of an apartment complex. It was at least fifty yards away—half the length of a football field. He hauled back, knowing he'd never hit it, let alone do any damage. It would just feel good to throw something.

He loosed it, pitching hard. The brick hit the dumpster's front edge with a *clang*. It jumped back three feet, at an angle. The brick shattered into smithereens, clay dust and pieces flying. He'd put a dent the size of a trash can lid in the front of it. He walked toward it, mesmerized.

"What'd you do that for?"

His sister, Dana, marched up behind him. At ten years old, she usually tried to act like Mom. She had his same hair color, as light as sun-bleached wheat, only her eyes were brown. She was sharp in every way.

"I didn't mean to. I didn't think I threw it that hard. Don't tell Mom," he added. Sudden elation washed out his anger. He let out a *whoop*. "Did you see how far it went? I mean, looka that! And you should've seen how I made the Big Butt Gang run!"

"So what? They just wrecked your iPod. Why aren't you upset?"

That halted him, and he pondered. "I dunno. I feel great."

He did. Energy seemed to be building inside. He suddenly felt as though he could win at anything he tried.

Dana marched on, scornful. "I'm not going all freakazoid when I'm a teenager."

She had her back to him, which meant she missed it when a sudden, sun-bright glow burst from inside Jeremy, turning him white-hot to look at, fading as quickly as it came. Jeremy shaded his eyes and glanced at the sun, wondering if the sudden light came from a sunspot or something.

He walked Dana home from school and left her doing homework. Mom was sleeping—she worked nights. If Dana needed help with math or anything she could always ask Mrs. Junge, a retired teacher who lived across the hall and loved questions on anything having to do with schoolwork. She also loved gossip, which drove Mom nuts.

He crossed the grass courtyard with apartments around it in a square "U." They were older two-stories of dull tan brick with black, wrought-iron rails on the patios of both floors. His family's unit was on the other side of the building in the center as he faced the "U." The small city park beyond it had tennis courts, a playground, and a scattering of trees.

He reached the tallest of the red oaks alongside the building, a strong old thing with branches larger than most tree trunks. It had to be over a hundred years old, taller than the apartments by half. He had a crazy urge to make a leap for the "Y" even though it was twenty feet up. He felt as though he could fly.

So, making sure no one was watching him, he made a run and a hard leap, his arms stretched up.

Sa-whoosh! He went up and up and *up!* He caught a wad of slender branches near the top and planted his feet on a limb that bowed under his weight but held, barely. He stood swaying, clutching the upper branches with both hands, crushing twigs, grappling at the branch beneath him with his toes. He leaned toward the trunk and took a death hold on it, gasping out tiny squeaks of fright when he really needed to scream.

He slithered and clawed his way down to a larger branch sure to hold his weight and took in the fact that he'd jumped eighty feet up. Even here, he stood higher than the roof of his apartment building.

He climbed down to the "Y" and dropped, landing lightly because he wanted to. He was still scared, not because he could've fallen and died, but because somehow he knew he wouldn't have fallen.

He had to test it. In a near frenzy, he ran around the entire apartment complex, looking for a safe and secluded place from which to take off then get down again. If he was going crazy, he'd keep from killing himself by experiment.

He'd finally decided that the roof itself would work for a proving ground. But no, there were little kids and moms in the park by now. An older teen who lived below him skateboarded on the inside sidewalks. Grownups came home from work, walking into the foyer with grocery bags in their hands.

He ran down his street, turned at the next block, raced past houses and another set of apartments, and decided on the roof of a rental storage place. No one was around. Highway 10, a busy four-lane, had traffic screaming along it in the distance and at an angle to the storage units. He figured the drivers went too fast to take in a kid on the roof.

He made a short run and leaped. He shot upward, his heartbeat rising as fast as his body. He arced over the roof, his body horizontal to the ground, like Superman. No! He overshot! He stared, horrified, at the parking lot below and fought back toward the roof in the only way he could think of: he angled his arms like a little kid playing eagle.

He controlled his descent with his arms still outstretched, though it seemed that his mind was the main thing controlling him. He touched down on his toes and stood flatfooted on the roof.

He'd flown. He could *fly*.

The long, flat roof, the skyline and its clouds, and the distant traffic contracted and spun. His legs gave way. He plopped to his knees on hard tar embedded with gravel. He slapped out a hand to steady himself. The roof seemed to flip beneath him.

He slumped backward and blacked out. He defied anyone to keep from fainting after flying for the first time under his own power and pulling it off.

Chapter 2

GHOSTS AND DEMONS

H E CAME TO and lay staring at the sky, laughing softly. He was cold. He stood and launched himself, flying from one end of the roof to the other, twice. There was an alley-wide gap between rental buildings. He worked up his courage, his heart thudding in his ears, and leaped. He sailed over the gap, over the other roof, and out over the parking lot.

But someone stepped out of the rental office. He angled down swiftly, then swooped upward a few yards from the ground, thrust his feet down, and landed standing up, like a bird of prey pouncing. It seemed the natural thing to do, and it worked. The rental customer shot him an irritated look in passing, clearly startled by this kid that suddenly appeared at the edge of his vision.

Jeremy ran away without a word.

He landed on his balcony with a thump. Dana, studying at the kitchen counter, threw him an indignant look through the glass-and-screen sliding doors, and marched over to unlock them. He knew what disgusted her. He wasn't supposed to climb around on the fire escape stairs. Little did she know how he'd really gotten onto the balcony.

He slid the door and screen open, the warped frames jamming as they always did while squawking along the floor runners. The kitchen tile had scuffmarks and bare patches. Everything in this place had seen better days.

He stumbled inside and flopped into a kitchen chair. Dana stared at him. His hair must have looked like a squirrel's nest, and his eyes felt red from wind in his face.

"You look weird," she said, "like, all pale."

That filled him with sudden, electric fright. Hold on! He'd just flown. Humans didn't do that. What if … He frantically thought back to the afternoon attack. Had Sid and his boys killed him? No, he'd spoken to Dana. But what if he only thought she'd answered him?

He held out his arm to her. "Touch my arm. Is it solid?"

"*Mom!*"

"Don't wake her up!"

"She's already up, and you're sick. I brought in your backpack. You left it at the tree."

His eyes fell on the mess of wiring, computer chips, and plastic puzzle pieces that had been his iPod spread out on the counter.

"Maybe Grandma will get you a new one," said Dana switching from scolding to sympathy, "but I doubt it. Mom says Grandma and Grandpa aren't made of money either."

He was still too worried about being dead to care about the iPod.

Marcy Lapoint shuffled into the kitchen, dressed in Capri-length sweatpants and a t-shirt. She was the night manager at a restaurant, and she always slept for as many hours as the day allowed unless she had an appointment or something. Bags and dark circles under her eyes marred her face, and she had more wrinkles than most moms did in their early thirties. She hadn't had time to put on makeup yet or to curl her shoulder-length, russet brown hair. Still, she was pretty.

"Did you yell, Dana?" she asked. She advanced on them, smiling, and gave them each a hello kiss on the face. Jeremy flinched to her touch. She studied his face, frowning.

She clamped her hand on his forehead. "No fever."

"Am I cold?"

"Don't you feel well?"

She pressed her fingers to his face and neck, looking for swollen glands. She always did that when she thought he was sick. He touched her arm and found that his hand felt as warm and firm as her forearm. Relief flushed through him.

"I'm fine," he said.

They let go of each other. "How was your—" Her eyes drifted to the counter and the demolished iPod. "Oh, no. Jeremy! What happened?"

"Sid Lundahl's gang did it," said Dana. She made a face in her disgust.

Mom's face tightened. "That's terrible! What's with the school-ground monitors? Were they on coffee break? I'm calling the school."

"Mom, don't. Please? It's okay."

She marched into the living room for a tissue, her voice easily carrying back to them.

"No, it's not. This is ridiculous. Kids wrecking other kids' things! Do they think we can just go buy another one? I s'pose that's what Sid's dad does. 'Oh, no big deal. We buy our kids two-hundred-dollar gadgets every week.' That Sid should do jail time."

She didn't come back right away. Jeremy, listening hard, caught the worst sounds he knew. They always made him feel sick and sad ... pulsing fast breaths pushed out of a body and shaking breaths pulled in. Mom was crying.

He tiptoed to the door, Dana following his cue, at his side. Mom sat hunched on the couch, a tissue to her face. They watched in frozen sympathy until

Dana broke loose, strode to the couch, and rubbed Mom's shoulder. Mom blindly put an arm about her waist.

A broken iPod wasn't enough to make her cry, just by itself. On a hunch, Jeremy hustled back to the counter and looked through the stack of mail until he found an opened, empty envelope marked "Stillwater Correctional Facility."

He rifled through more papers. Mom came into the kitchen, her bout of crying already over, her arm about Dana's waist.

"The letter's not on the counter."

"What did it say?" he asked her, though he already guessed.

"Dad didn't make parole again."

Jeremy balled up the envelope and threw it, not caring where it landed.

"They won't let him out?" asked Dana, suddenly sounding younger. "Now he won't be home for Christmas."

She buried her face in Mom's shoulder. Mom rubbed her back.

Jeremy towed the waste paper basket over to the counter and hand-swept the wrecked iPod into it.

Anoka Middle School was an older, single-story building with many halls and ramps, huge, and packed with kids. They tried to brighten it by painting the walls royal blue halfway up and white the rest of the way. They posted "Respect" banners and inspirational posters all over the place. No one saw them anymore.

Jeremy hurried in the front door with a throng of other young teens, trying to put the same bored look on his face that everyone wore.

A harried school secretary wrote passes and handed them through a slot in the main office's Plexiglas window as a dozen kids waited in line for them. Principal Howard Pollaski stood in his office doorway watching the tide pour in. He was tall with a huge bald spot on the top of his head, and his tie and slacks were always too short.

Jeremy turned left into the seventh grade hallway and made for his locker at the far end. Five Goths lolled near the science room dressed all in black from their baggy pants-with-chains to their fingernails and dyed hair. Their leader wore a pentagram on a leather cord around her neck. They scorned everyone and knew very well that they were scary.

Jeremy didn't look their way. Then someone shoved him hard, sending him stumbling into the Goth leader. He stomped on her foot. She yelped in pain. "Look out, you dumb—!"

"He-e-e-y, let's watch the language, people," sang out Pollaski.

Jeremy regained his balance in time to see the backs of Sid and his boys laughing as they moved on.

Jeremy gave the Goth leader a hasty apology. "Hey, sorry. I was pushed."

She waved him off, her friends snickering. He turned away, but then a different sort of laughter suddenly came from their midst, loud and hissing, like a snake venting a burst of steam. He couldn't help looking back at them.

A creature now stood amidst the Goths. It was the size of an orangutan, with a scaly gray hide, long claws, and fangs in an ape-like face. It wore a black tunic with a dagger on its belt. Jeremy froze, horrified, making kids step around him.

The demon narrowed its yellow eyes at him. "You can see me, eh?" it rasped, in a voice that sounded like sliding gravel. "Let's see how fast you can run!"

It lunged at him. Jeremy cried out and sprinted all-out for the side hall. The Goths burst into amazed laughter. Teens scuttled out of his way, bumping into each other, turning the influx of students into a traffic jam.

"Settle down, people!" said Pollaski. He could be loud even if he wasn't shouting.

The thing nearly had him, and then Pollaski stepped in Jeremy's way! He tried to duck around him but ran into him instead. Pollaski caught his shoulders.

The demon struck. Jeremy felt a hot, cutting pain in his back and heard his shirt rip. Pollaski was so surprised, he let go.

Meanwhile, the demon had its own problems. Something unseen to Jeremy grabbed it by the scruff and threw it backwards at least twenty feet. It landed, snarling.

"Mind your own business, you … !" It leaped high in the air, as though flying over something in its way.

Pollaski reached for Jeremy's forearm to walk him to his office, but Jeremy took off again.

The side hall was packed with kids. He darted through them, drawing yells of disgust. Jeremy glanced back to see the demon soaring after him like a pterodactyl, its black, leathery wings flapping hard. *Whomp, whomp, whomp.*

He raced on, in full panic. The English 1-A door opened a little. The demon reached out its claws. Jeremy grabbed the door handle and jerked it open. It was all he could think of to do.

The demon ran headlong into it, *wham,* and hit the hall floor with a thud.

A warm, masculine voice laughed near his ear. "Well done!" said the speaker. "Caught him by surprise."

Jeremy peered about him, trying to locate the man. Who else could see the monster, when everyone stared at him as though it wasn't there? He didn't have much time to look. The demon kicked the door shut and faced him with its fists clenched, roaring like an alligator.

"Fly," said the voice.

Jeremy galloped away, making for the outside doors at the end of the hall. The creature surged in the air after him.

"Don't run. *Fly.*"

Jeremy felt a strong hand catch hold of the back of his shirt while another caught him under the arm. But he could see no one touching him. The hands hoisted him halfway to the ceiling. "I'm throwing you," said the voice, "for a head start. On your own now …"

The hands propelled him into the air. He sailed along the ceiling, yelling all the way. He couldn't help it.

Boys shouted. Girls screamed. An eighth-grade girl flipped open her cell phone and took photos.

The outside doors were closed! If he landed, the demon would pounce on him like a hawk on a mouse.

Then the right-hand door burst open by itself. He sailed through the frame, and it closed fast again, as though someone pulled it shut. This time the demon was ready for it and passed clean through the door as though it were a ghost.

No one needed to tell Jeremy to fly as fast as he could. He passed the flagpole, gaining height.

The creature put on a burst of speed. So did Jeremy. It strained to grab him. Jeremy zigzagged and spun. They soared higher. All he could see was sky and distant clouds.

"*Raugh!*" The demon was in his face! Somehow, it had shot ahead of him. Jeremy arced to the right and wet, thick fog surrounded him. *What?* He had flown into a cloud.

The white mist darkened to charcoal gray. The demon had followed him in. Jeremy raced on, having no idea if he was going up, down, or sideways. He glanced behind. The creature's grasping claws, curved like talons, were inches from his heel. He pushed himself with all his speed toward the thickest part of the cloud, and it was suddenly lit as if by searchlights in the mist.

A man-shaped being flared hot white in front of him. He arced around Jeremy, cutting between him and the monster. He hit it with the golden shield he bore, sending the creature backwards end-over-end.

The demon spread its wings hard and stopped, but only for a breath. With a screech of rage, it launched at the lighted man.

He looked as young as a man could be; twenty years old, if he was human, which he clearly was not. He brandished a sword, yellow flames running along the blade like loose electricity. He leaped. The creature passed under him. He flipped head-down like an Olympic diver and took a two-armed swipe with the sword, lopping off the demon's left wing.

The leathery thing spun downward like one of those helicopter box elder seeds Jeremy used to play with in the back yard. The creature roared and made a grab at the young man's foot.

"You don't give up, do you?" the man said, in the golden-toned voice Jeremy already knew. "What next? Your head?"

The monster dropped, flapping erratically like a bat with a broken wing. The cloud turned pure white again.

Jeremy suddenly realized he was hovering. He could feel the things on his shoulders, flapping gently, lit with a gentle glow of their own. He had wings; but of light, not feathers.

So did the young man. He eased back his brightness until he looked almost human. He sheathed his sword and drew face-to-face, yet not so close that they could touch. He seemed to know that Jeremy needed space right now, and he was smiling.

He looked like every angel Jeremy had ever seen in paintings. His wings were golden-colored and not quite solid, open, and flapping easily on either side of his shoulders. He had golden-brown hair hanging to his shoulders. His face was smooth, the bones fine, and his eyes shone with such a light blue they were almost clear.

He wore a white, one-piece thing that had long, open sleeves and a woven belt of gold at the front. A knotted cloth covered the buckle. The puffed-out pants, gathered in folds along the insides of his legs, ended in angled openings above his knees. It looked like a mixture of a karate outfit and a graduation gown.

Then the angel untied the white knot at his belt. The fabric loosened and dropped to hang straight down, almost to his sandals. It turned out to be a one-piece robe that he had pulled up between his legs from front to back, the hem stretched around each side of his waist and tied at the front.

Jeremy caught himself in a frown, wondering what made him dwell on such a dumb thing at a time like this.

"You have many questions, Jeremy. I know you do," said the angel.

Chapter 3

THE NEPHILIM

JEREMY FOLLOWED THE angel out of the cloud, the sun warming him the instant they cleared the mist. Anoka spread below them like a jigsaw puzzle, the Mississippi River a wide, shiny band to the west.

The angel came alongside him. "My name is Asiel," he said. He soared easily.

It was a stupid question, but Jeremy asked it anyway. "What are you, exactly?"

"You already know."

Fright as cold as the mist shot through him. He halted, hovering. "Oh-h-h, man! I am dead, then. That's why things have gone all weird. Am I an angel, too?"

"Why do humans think they'll change into us when they die? Would a cat become a dog? No, you're a Nephilim."

"But I'm alive?"

"Of course."

Jeremy gave a high squeak of a laugh and felt like he was breathing again.

"You are human and angel, both. Read of your kind in the Holy Scriptures. Genesis, the sixth chapter, and Numbers, the thirteenth chapter. The Nephilim were born in the days before Noah, when my kind made women their wives."

"Angels and women? Were they good marriages?"

"The Lord of Hosts didn't allow it for long. Their children, the Nephilim, would've dominated the world. The few there were became 'heroes of old,' the Scriptures say. They died in the course of time, their souls going on to their chosen places. 'Tis the way for all who are mortal, even if only in part. However, the Nephilim men and women didn't decay as a pure human does. Their flesh was infused with partial immortality, although their souls were long gone. They lay in their tombs looking as they had in life for ages and ages, but of course, they will never live again."

Asiel flew on, angling them downward well below the clouds. "It was war that exposed the bodies. In the ancient city where the Nephilim lay, invading armies built siege ramps, broke the outer walls, and finished the work with axes and fire. The invaders wrecked the tombs. The survivors, burying their dead, came upon their ancestors who should have been bones and dust but looked, instead, as sleepers do.

"The descendents of the Nephilim held the bodies in awe and terror. They built new tombs strongly hidden. They wrote of them in pictures, held as holy, for this was before written words."

"Egyptians?" asked Jeremy.

"No. The Pharaohs' bodies are hard leather and bones now. The Nephilim still look asleep."

"Now? They're still around?"

"Yes. And their legend lives on, though it's known to a bare few. Some of those few would kill the legend at all costs, for they don't want others to believe it, even as they seek the Nephilim for themselves."

"What for? Have they found them?"

"I've told you all I know."

"Yeah, but how did I get like this?"

"Too much knowledge now will be dangerous for you."

"Dangerous?" echoed Jeremy.

"Seek the truth at the proper time—and the One who gives it. The angel in your kind longs to serve Him. The human … has a fight on his hands."

That stunned Jeremy enough to make him brake with his wings again. What Asiel just said sent shock waves through him. "Are you … talking about … God?" He fought to control his breathing and poured out a babble of words. "Well, Mom took us to church when we were little, but now she has to work Sundays, and Dad always said he'd rather fish. Are you telling me that God is really *real*?"

Jeremy didn't know what he believed. Now, it seemed, he'd *have* to know. How could you argue about religion with an angel? Asiel, meanwhile, frowned a silent question at him: *how can you even ask?*

He led them onward. "I have one more thing to tell you. You're not alone. There are two hundred and thirty of you in Europe, Canada, and America. You are the new Nephilim. Many will delight in you. Many will hate you heartily."

"Why?"

"Because you show them living truth."

Jeremy was so confused by now, his head hurt. He recognized Anoka Middle School, growing larger as they neared it. A straggling line of girls in yellow phys-ed uniforms jogged the track. Boys warmed up nearby. "They saw me fly. What do I tell them?"

"As much of the truth as you must."

That drew a groan from him. "Don't angels ever give straight answers?"

"Will yourself to go invisible," said Asiel, and promptly disappeared to Jeremy's sight.

Jeremy blinked, amazed. *Go invisible,* he ordered himself.

He didn't feel any different. Then he looked at his hands. *What hands?* "This is too weird!" he blurted out. "I can feel my hands move, but I can't see them!"

"Land near the front entrance."

They were tree height above the ground. Jeremy had landed enough to know how to slow himself, rise up a little, and touch down. "Yeah, but, how do I judge it? I can't see my feet!"

His feet slapped down harder than he wanted them to. His knees buckled, and he stumbled, falling to his hands and knees with a slap of palms and a grunt that slowed down a mom hurrying into the school. She saw no one, of course, and picked up her pace at once, disappearing through the doors.

Jeremy stood in Mr. Pollaski's office, waiting as the principal sat at his cluttered desk, working at his laptop. At last, he seemed to find what he wanted onscreen and set his full attention on Jeremy. He was dangerously angry.

"Turn," he said.

Jeremy obeyed. The plate-sized hole in his shirt made his back feel chilly. The scratches were stinging. The dried blood pulled at his skin.

"What did you use? Cables?"

Jeremy faced him again. *As much of the truth as I must.* "There were these … things on my back."

"Who helped you?"

Jeremy couldn't possibly answer that. He gave a weak shrug.

Pollaski turned the laptop and let Jeremy see a photo of himself soaring along the school ceiling. He stayed silent. Nothing else was safe.

"Whoever took this downloaded it to the Internet in a matter of five minutes." Pollaski let that hang.

"I'd congratulate you on pulling off a great stunt if you hadn't gotten hurt. Didn't you realize you were endangering yourself and others on campus? What if your cables had broken at a hundred feet up?"

He spun his laptop back to face him, clicking off the picture with the speed of anger. "You're in detention for the rest of the day. And this may earn you a suspension."

Then he sighed and loosened up, a little. "Let's get you to the nurse."

Classes had just let out by the noises drifting in the door. Mr. Pollaski led the way down the busy hall. They'd nearly reached the nurse's office when Sid's too-well-known voice fired at Jeremy's back like a rifle shot. "Up in the sky! It's jailbird!"

By that night, the photo made the major news websites. Jeremy sat at the desk, Dana standing at his shoulder, both of them staring at the old desktop computer. "Gol, Jeremy!" she breathed.

Mom paced the kitchen, talking on the cell phone. He squirmed at the agitation in her voice. "It's on what? The Internet?"

She rushed into the front room. Jeremy was tempted to log out, but he kept the mouse still and let her gaze, frowning. They'd featured his flying-through-the-hall picture in the news site's "Oddities" section. At least it wasn't the top news story. Bold text under the photo said, "Can 13-year-old Jeremy Lapoint fly? Witnesses say he did. *More*."

Mom clicked on the link button and read in silence, clenching her fingers, the muscles on her forearms tightening into cords. She was coming to a boil. He headed her off.

"Mom, I've got something to tell you."

After Jeremy explained that he was part angel while still human, Mom sat on the couch in rigid silence. Dana, beside her, got the giggles, but she squeaked in astonishment when he rose to the ceiling. He flew into the kitchen and back, touching down gently.

"See my wings? They only show up when I need to fly. I'm glad or I'd get beat up for wearing them. They're not like feathers, though, just kind of like thick light."

Mom's eyes dilated, and her face went white. "Mom? Mm-maybe you'd better put your head down. Mom?"

Her eyes rolled. She slumped, about to fall off the couch. He caught her by the shoulders and rested her sideways. Dana grabbed a sofa pillow for her head while he brought up her feet.

Dana was crying. "Go get Mrs. Junge!"

"No way!"

Asiel appeared, but Dana didn't see him.

"Wet a cloth and lay it on her forehead," said the angel.

"Okay. Warm or cold water?" Jeremy asked, rushing to the kitchen.

"Cold."

"Wh-who are you talking t-to?" Dana called to him.

"My guardian angel. He doesn't want you to see him. Don't ask me why. His name is Asiel." He soaked a cloth under the tap, wrung it, and hurried back.

Dana stared about her, wide-eyed. "H-hello, Angel," she murmured.

Asiel bowed to her.

Mom moaned, her eyes moving under their lids in her fight to open them. He placed the cold cloth on her forehead, hoping the shock would help her. It worked. She opened her eyes, apologizing, and thanked them for taking care of her. He and Dana took hold of her hands. Asiel disappeared again.

Jeremy felt warm with shame. "I shouldn't have been such a show off."

"And how else would we have believed?"

Mom asked him to bring her a blanket from the linen closet. She gave the washcloth to Dana who scooted to the kitchen with it. He ran down the hallway and was back in thirty seconds with a quilt. Dana came back with a glass of water.

He covered her. Mom raised her head and took a long drink, breaking into a smile. Her eyes grew bright and red patches formed in her cheeks. She let

Dana put the glass on the coffee table and reached for Jeremy. "You are a miracle!" she blurted out, crushing him with a hug. "Can you get my Bible? I think it's on the shelf in my closet."

He sprang away again, and found it easily, blowing the dust off its cover. He'd reached her doorway when she called out another question. "What are you called again?"

He stepped into the hall, grinning. "I'm a Nephilim!"

Chapter 4

SUSPENSION

THANKSGIVING DAY ARRIVED and Pollaski had not suspended Jeremy, a fact for which he was very thankful. The gloom that had hung over his family for the past four years as they faced the holidays without Dad wasn't as heavy this year. Jeremy did notice Mom looking at Dad's picture, her eyes sad. She popped out of it when she became aware of him, and simply said, "I wish your dad could see you now."

So did Jeremy. Even so, the secret excitement of his new abilities added to the anticipation of Christmas. Mom liked to decorate early. Two days before Thanksgiving, lights and evergreen branches hung on the windows—even the highest—no ladder needed. He hovered, easily placing the star on the top of the artificial Christmas tree they'd used for years. Mom and Dana applauded.

They spent Thanksgiving Day at Grandma and Grandpa's, their little three-bedroom house stuffed with relatives. Dana was in her glory, nearly all of their cousins being girls around her age. Their one boy cousin was only ten months old. Not exactly someone Jeremy could play a video game with, and he'd die before he played Barbies.

Uncle Charlie, Mom's youngest brother, nineteen years old and home from college, straggled in an hour after everyone else had arrived, and to Jeremy's warm surprise, sought him out.

"The grownups will just ooh and ah at how tall I am and ask me what I'm majoring in," he griped, mildly, "like it isn't the twentieth time I've told them. So, what's new with you?"

Jeremy longed to tell him, but Mom warned him not to for the time being. "Not that much," he said.

"You liking school?"

He shrugged. Charlie didn't dwell on it. Jeremy's heart gave a leap as he pulled out two joysticks from his closet and plugged them into his computer. Charlie left it up to him to pick the game. He chose "Flying Aces."

Jeremy was old enough now to sit at the dining table with the grownups, Charlie at his shoulder. Grandma's turkey dinner was one of his favorite meals in the world: stacks of turkey, no limits on the mashed potatoes, and warm crescent rolls. He even liked the candied carrots, though he'd pass on the stuffing, and her gravy! It had to be the best tasting in the world. It had to be.

Grandpa came in with the sliced turkey mounded on a platter as big as a Roman shield. He set it down on the serving counter as the grownups shushed the kids, and Grandma, Mom, and Jeremy's three aunts scurried in from the last-second things they were doing. Mom plunked in the empty chair by Jeremy, and they bowed their heads for grace.

Grandpa did the praying, of course. He cleared his voice, as he always did, growing misty when he thanked God for his family. He was softhearted. He also had the habit of wiping his nose on a cloth hanky and stuffing it in his back pocket, which always grossed Jeremy out.

He sat to Mom's left and Dana stood to her right. She'd join the cousins at the kids' table after grace. Mom squeezed her kids' hands all through the prayer, but she also had to snatch her napkin and wipe the tears that wanted to trickle from her eyes. She'd always have sorrow mixed with joy until Dad came home.

Jeremy missed him, too. He lifted a brief, silent prayer of his own for Dad to have a good Thanksgiving, somehow. Then he offered a shy "Thank-you" for the gifts he'd been given, from the warm and normal to the wild and unbelievable. Even such a short prayer made him feel hot from head to toe. He hoped God didn't mind the awkwardness.

Grandpa ended with a hearty, "Amen!" Everyone lifted their heads as they murmured the word. Mom gave her kids hugs, and it was time to dig in.

Mom had to work the next night. Jeremy and Dana cleaned the apartment while she got some extra sleep. She and Dana planned to bake cookies that afternoon. Dana did the dusting and swept the floors while Jeremy cleaned the bathroom, his room, and vacuumed. He did a good job because it was easy to do so. Mom called it another miracle.

He was in the mood to practice flying after lunch. Asiel appeared, ready to train him. At first, Mom argued. He'd be gone all day with a being she couldn't see, yet she was supposed to entrust her son to him? Gradually, she grew still. "I think I feel him," she said, her voice trembling. "It's very peaceful in here."

Asiel was standing next to her.

"He says we'll be back by our suppertime, and it's God's peace that you feel."

They left, walking side-by-side. The day was cloudy and cold with a light wind. Jeremy wore his winter jacket and had a cap and gloves in his pockets. He knew what the wind chill in November would feel like high above the Twin Cities.

They reached the park, both of them invisible. People passed within a few feet, taking no notice of them even when he and Asiel talked. "They can't hear us, either?" asked Jeremy. "How come?"

"We don't wish to be heard."

Asiel stopped at the side of the men's restroom, the brick wall decorated with a huge Christmas wreath. A man and a three-year-old boy passed them, trotting toward the door. The child squirm danced in his need to go. Would they take off from here?

"Now, first lesson," began Asiel, "passing through walls. Your clothes will pass through because they're on your person. But any object of this realm that you're carrying, such as a box, will not."

Jeremy was thunderstruck. "We can go through *walls?*"

"And any other solid barrier. You must respect their privacy, of course."

"Hee-yeah!" he blustered, going hot in the face. "How does it work, though? Will I go ghosty?"

"Ghosty?"

"See-through. I dunno."

Jeremy stared at the wall in a sweat.

"What do you fear?" Asiel asked him.

"What if my brain freaks, and I go solid, like, halfway though?"

"How very like the apostle Peter." Asiel didn't give Jeremy's doubts the time of day, but walked through the wall.

Jeremy worked up his courage as though prepping to dive off the high board. "Okay, one, two, three … !" But he stopped with his nose an inch from the bricks. Their rough faces looked sharp!

"One, two, *three!* Okay, now I'm going to move. One, two—"

Asiel's hand and arm came back through the wall, caught him by the jacket front, and pulled him through.

They spent the afternoon flying, Jeremy glad to have his cap and gloves. The strong wind up high made his eyes water. Asiel taught him how to find giant swirls, called air columns, spinning up from the earth. Eagles and hawks used these to circle. But he also learned to fly into the wind, his arms outstretched and tight to his lowered head, his eyes lifted to look ahead. He had power within to outdo the wind, Asiel told him. It was tiring, though, with fast-growing aches rolling along his arms, neck, and back.

Asiel showed him how to angle his wings for fast turning and spinning. He taught him to draw one wing in for a wingover roll, tucking them in tightly against the wind. With the wind, they opened them just enough to race at jet speed.

Darkness came early this time of year. It was only six o'clock by Jeremy's watch when Asiel headed them back home, yet full night was upon them. They'd nearly reached Minneapolis. The IDS Tower, the shorter skyscrapers, streetlights, and Christmas lights made downtown look bright and warm, lighting the low clouds with a dim glow of gold.

But the air was freezing. Jeremy wanted hot cocoa and supper, in that order. Asiel assured him he'd be on time. They turned north, toward home, the wind to their backs. Jeremy's icy face suddenly felt warm and there was no roar in his ears. The wind pushed him to a screaming speed. He couldn't believe he'd make it home in half-an-hour.

Asiel, at his side, grinned. "Top of your speed! And go bright!" Asiel clamped his arms to his ears and surged ahead. He went incandescent as he had been when Jeremy first met him.

Jeremy desired the same thing. Energy rose in his core and burst forth as blazing white light. They doubled their speed. He had to yell to the rush of it. "Ya-a-a-a-h-h-h!"

Asiel laughed.

Far below, in the northern suburb of Coon Rapids, a backyard astronomer lowered his binoculars and excitedly jotted a note in his journal: "Unusual. Two meteorites at once."

Monday brought school again. Sid and company taunted him, tripped him, and made his life miserable in a dozen other ways. He'd about had it by phys-ed, third hour. The day was chilly and overcast, one of the last in which they'd play soccer before winter really hit.

Mr. Grant, the head of the athletics department, stood watching. He was medium in height and broad-of-everything. Young, buff Mr. Chilson warmed them up and started the game—orange net vests versus those not wearing them. He put Jeremy on the latter team, stuck in the back as a guard, with Chad playing the same position, unfortunately.

"Super sleaze ball!" Chad taunted him. "Do you like pain?"

Fun question. Sid played midfield for the other team. He stole the ball away from one of his own forwards and motored downfield in spite of his teammates yelling at him. Players on both sides tried to steal it and couldn't. In Sid's case, size outdid skill.

Jeremy tensed. Sid's cronies gathered around him, whether they were in position or not. They hemmed him in. He wanted to fly away, but knew better than to do such a display again.

Sid neared him and suddenly scooped up the ball and threw it hard in Jeremy's face. It crunched against his nose and lips. He saw stars and tasted blood. He turned away, doubling over, cupping his hands to his face.

Someone with beefy hands and a vise grip caught Jeremy's wrists and yanked them back, and planted his knee in the middle of his back, keeping him from straightening. It was Chad. Jeremy recognized his beat up skater shoes.

Sid moved in to knee him in the face. Jeremy gave a strangled yell, twisted away from Chad, and threw him. Chad flew twenty feet through the air, his arms flailing, and came down on one foot before he flopped in the grass and rolled another ten feet.

That wasn't the worst of it. Jeremy shone as bright as a stadium light. The other boys yelled and spun away. Mr. Chilson, running and blowing his whistle, wheeled away shielding his eyes, the whistle dropping from his lips.

Jeremy froze, mortified. Fear and humiliation cooled his fury in the instant. The light died, and he was his plain self again. Only how would he get out of this one?

The other players stared at him like he was a phantom. Mr. Grant stood rooted in the silence, but it didn't last. Chad moaned in pain. That launched Mr. Grant into action. He strode over to him. Chad clutched his right arm, which had gone as red as if it were sunburned. It trembled, swelling at the wrist like there was a tennis ball under his skin.

"That's a break," said Grant. "Alec! Marty! Get him to the nurse's office. Can you stand?"

Chad sat up, Grant helping him. He struggled to his feet, his face as red as his arm, battling off tears of pain. "I'll break something of yours, Lapoint!"

"All right, get him in," said Grant. Alec and two others escorted him away.

Grant rounded on Jeremy. "What happened here?"

"I'b really zorry I puzhed Jad zo hard," Jeremy began, his swelling lips garbling his words. "I didn't bean to. Zid and hiz friendz ganged ub on be."

Blood dripped off his chin. Mr. Chilson trotted up with a first-aid kit and handed Jeremy a swath of gauze to press to his lips and nose.

"I kicked the ball in Lapoint's face by accident, Coach," countered Sid, sounding reasonable. "He went ballistic."

"He didn't kigg it! He threw it."

"No way! You're delusional …"

"Somebody else must hab seen it. Adybody … ?"

Grant cut him off harshly. "That's enough! You have seriously injured another student. We're going to see Mr. Pollaski. Mr. Chilson, continue the game."

He waited for Jeremy to take the lead, then marched after him. Jeremy gave a last look behind and saw Sid and company exchange subtle grins. The injustice of it piled in on him. No, of course Grant wasn't going to ask if anyone else had seen what really happened. That would turn a single incident that he could clamp on and get over with into an investigation in which he would have to question his class and get angry parents involved.

Too much work. Easier to just call Jeremy a liar. Sid must've banked on Grant's laziness. However, the coach still had uncomfortable things to deal with. Most of the boys were upset, their minds on anything but the soccer game.

"Coach," yelled out a boy named Fred. "Did you see the light that came off him? Did you?"

Grant had a ready answer that he bellowed back in his disgust (and bewilderment, if he would admit it). "That was the sun hitting him through a break in the clouds. And that's all! Got it? Mr. Chilson … !"

Chilson blew the whistle. The game started again. Grant nodded curtly at Jeremy to keep walking. Jeremy knew one thing—he was in serious trouble. He only hoped the incident wouldn't make the Internet news sites again or worse.

Mr. Pollaski called Mom almost the minute Jeremy and Dana got home from school. He listened from the hallway, wincing as her voice grew louder and louder. "A week! Mr. Pollaski, it was an accident. He didn't know his own strength. But there must be allowances for … This is so unfair!"

She hung up. Jeremy stomped into the front room as she stalked from the kitchen, the cell phone forgotten in her hand. He headed off her lecture with his own tirade. "I'm suspended for a week? I knew it! Grant's too lazy to ask around if anybody saw what really happened. It's so much easier just to dump it all on me. What a—"

"Watch what you say about a teacher," she snapped.

"I'm scared. What if the guys who saw me go bright talk to … people?"

The phone rang in her hand, startling them both. Mom took a second to get her breath back and mellow her voice. "Hello, Mrs. Junge," she began, her automatic smile as plastic as a doll's. "Oh, we're fine." The smile was gone in the next instant. "What's going on outside?" she demanded, the edge right back in her voice. "No, I have no idea why a crowd has gathered in the parking lot."

That sent Jeremy running to the kitchen.

"Reporters?" he heard her ask, her voice sharp. She forced it back to pleasant. "Yes … uh-huh … Yes, thanks for telling me, Mrs. Junge …"

She was right behind him, punching off the phone. Dana scuttled in silently, in stocking feet. Jeremy stood frozen at the windows, feeling like his heart had dropped to his heels. News station vans and cars took up half the parking lot, making residents park elsewhere than their numbered stalls. They weren't happy, but they obviously didn't dare complain. They beat it into the building or stood gaping.

Technical crews hustled to set up equipment. News teams formed attack groups.

A reporter spotted him. Three TV channel crews raced toward the balcony.

"Shut the window!" hissed Mom.

He frantically pushed the screen out of the way, *sque-e-ek*. The glass window fought as he pulled it, bouncing in the track. Mom rushed to help him, dropping to her knees.

Lee Englestad was Channel 5's top news reporter/announcer for twenty years running. He had dignified, silver hair and a young man's build, and loosed a bellow before Mom and Jeremy could quite get the window shut. "Jeremy! Did you fly? And what made you go so bright your classmates couldn't look at you? They say you're an alien. What do you say?"

That shocked Jeremy to his toenails. His head flew up from bending over the stubborn window. He found himself staring, horrified, at the single, enormous eyes of a dozen cameras of both types—photo and video. Mom leaped into action, yanking the vertical blinds across the sliding doors, then herded Jeremy and Dana out of the kitchen before the blinds stopped swaying.

Chapter 5

THE INVITATION

AROUND FIVE-THIRTY, JEREMY sat on the couch studying science getting nothing out of it. Reporters had been ringing the doorbell at about ten-minute intervals since they'd gotten here. Mom got ready for work, muttering a lot as she strode between her room and the bathroom. She was close to exploding.

She hurried into the kitchen to start supper. Jeremy re-read a paragraph about cellular mitosis for the third time, and he still had no idea what it meant. A loud voice carried in from the hallway, closed door notwithstanding. "Excuse me! I need to get through."

It was a woman. The doorbell rang once more, and she outright bellowed. "Express mail delivery!"

Mom hurried from the kitchen. She unlocked and unchained the door opening it just enough to stick her arm out to reach for the package. The reporters swarmed like jackals, their voices a babble of yelling.

She pulled in the package and tried to shut the door. Someone large and strong blocked it. "You—" she began, fuming. The blocker would push it open in the next half-second, and they'd be in.

Jeremy hopped to the rescue, catching a glimpse of the man with his shoulder to the door—young, chunky, and grinning like a defensive tackle about to sack the quarterback. Jeremy planted his hands on their side of the door and shoved it shut with a bang. The blocker gave a yelp that was sweet to hear. Stumbling footsteps told him the guy struggled to keep from falling.

A shout drowned out the reporters' voices. Jeremy and Mom knew that big voice well—Mr. Reye, the building's maintenance man, had arrived. Maybe ten years younger than Grandpa, his face turned a gorgeous red when he was angry. Not that he'd ever been mad at Mom or her kids, but troublemakers got their earwax melted. Come to think of it, he'd caught Jeremy climbing on the fire escape, once …

Mr. Reye must have been apple-colored now. "If you people don't clear out in five minutes, I'm calling the police!"

Mom clicked the bolt shut and re-attached the chain with shaking hands. She hurried to her bedroom, too agitated to remember to thank Jeremy for saving them from invasion. That steamed him. Not that he was angry with her. What was up with these people, stressing her out like this! How would they like it if somebody harassed them?

That gave him an idea he couldn't resist. He went invisible.

He passed into the hallway. The reporters hadn't budged.

"All right, then," declared Mr. Reye, his face scarlet. He strode to his apartment.

Jeremy tiptoed to Lee Englestad and touched him in the side; not hard, but enough to make sure he felt it.

"Ay!" croaked Englestad, flinching. "Somebody jabbed me!"

Jeremy followed that with a slap at the bill of the Twins baseball cap Englestad's camera operator wore—the big guy who had blocked the door against Mom. It flew off his head. They both exclaimed over that one, the operator reaching for his head. He was in his early twenties, with spiky blond hair, and an out-of-shape football tackle's build.

The other reporters and crew stared while the operators readied their cameras.

He didn't dare play around with the large, expensive-looking video cam the operator shouldered.

However, the guy also had a small photo camera dangling on his left wrist. This was going to be tricky.

Jeremy held his breath and took a firm grip on the cord. He whisked it off the guy's wrist and dangled it in front of his astonished eyes, then set it gently on the floor before other camera people could get a focus on it. He tugged it along the carpet like a kid with a pull toy, once again dropping the cord just as the operators got a fix on it.

Their exclamations and expletives made it hard not to burst out laughing. He tiptoed away before someone bumped into him.

A middle-aged, paunchy Anoka Police Officer came striding up the stairs. "The owner wants you gone, ladies and gentlemen," he announced.

The reporters and crew filed toward the stairs, sharing their agitation none-too-quietly, none of it directed at the officer. Jeremy followed them, soft-footed. The beat-up old carpet helped him.

"What was that?" asked the camera operator, pausing on the first landing.

Englestad cast a look upwards, straight into Jeremy's eyes. "I wonder."

The Twins cap lay against a wall. Jeremy picked it up, the officer catching sight of it rising by itself. He changed from sternly businesslike to open-mouthed in astonishment. Jeremy tossed it at the operator, hitting his shoulder. He jerked, yelped, and snatched it off the floor, staring up wildly to meet eyes with the bewildered cop.

"Don't look at me," said the officer. "That thing flew by itself." He shook his head. "I been watchin' too many of them ghost hunter shows."

"I'm finding out everything I can about that kid," said Englestad, and went on his way.

The camera operator planted his cap on his large head and hurried down the stairs.

Inside the apartment, Dana stood by the door, staring at it as if monsters waited on the other side. Jeremy tickled her side. She shrieked and scuttled away. He broke out laughing.

"Did you do that to them?" Mom asked, demanding to know. "Where are you? I'm not talking to air!"

He plopped on the couch and materialized, still chuckling. "I didn't hurt anything. I just messed 'em up."

"Which means they'll be after us all the more. If you'd left them alone, the story would've died."

He switched to sullen. "I just wanted to lighten things up, and you have to spazz out."

She thrust the express mail letter in his face. It was a cardboard letter holder, addressed to him. He tore it open. Mom sat on the couch arm to read along with him. Dana scrambled onto the middle cushion and tried to make something of a letter that had way too many long words in it.

It had two pages with an important-looking letterhead at the top of each. The logo, a pen drawing, showed a teen boy and girl lifting off the ground, straining to fly upward. "What's the Higher Humanity Institute?" he asked.

"Something this Louisa Prouse wants you to join." Mom scanned ahead to learn the gist of the letter. "It's a 'refuge and learning center for the uniquely gifted.'" She had tight wrinkles at the corners of her mouth. She didn't like it.

"You mean teens that can fly?"

A photograph dropped from between the pages and landed facedown on the carpet. Jeremy and Dana dove for it. He beat her to it, but had the grace to hold it for Dana to see as he took his own long look. The girl in the picture had long, caramel-colored hair, snappy eyes, and a bright grin. She wore in-style jeans and a store-brand shirt.

But it was seeing her hovering at tree height that took his breath away. She had his same golden light-wings curving out from her upper back.

"I'm not alone," he breathed.

Mom gave the photo a glance, then read aloud from the beginning. "Dear Mrs. Lapoint and Jeremy, please let me introduce myself. I am Mrs. Louisa Prouse, and I know precisely what you're going through. My very own granddaughter, Rachel, is manifesting the same newfound, amazing abilities Jeremy has shown. I've included her picture."

She continued reading, silently, as Jeremy read for himself, still holding the photo. He'd hardly completed the next paragraph when Mom snorted. "Oh! What is that, a bribe?"

"Mom, do you always have to read ahead?"

She read aloud again. "I know what happened to you in school. Don't be alarmed by that. My staff and I watch the news for such incidents all around the country. I am an educator and leader in the American Education Foundation. I'll be Jeremy's advocate to Principal Pollaski and your school's Advisory Board to make sure nothing negative goes into his school records."

"That's a good thing, isn't it?"

Judging by the scowl Mom shot him, he'd best keep it at that.

"I'd like you to consider the Higher Humanity Institute as a better alternative for Jeremy." Mom pursed her lips and read in silence once more.

But neither of her kids could stand it.

"What's that mean?" Dana blurted out.

"What alternative?" asked Jeremy.

She ignored their questions. "Oh, no way! It's some old abandoned college, and she wants you to live there. This place will 'grant you a scholarship' and give you free room and board. Come on! What's her real agenda?"

Jeremy's heart rose. Get away from Anoka Middle School? He'd live in a prison in the Amazon jungle!

"Where?" asked Dana.

He beat Mom to the answer with a glance at the letterhead. "Along lovely Lake of the Ozarks."

"Podunk, Missouri," said Mom, sounding dangerous.

"Actually, the address is Leesville."

"You are not going."

Shocked anger flared in him. She was turning this perfect offer down just like that? "Why not?"

"It's too good. It sounds suspicious."

"It sounds cool!"

They locked eyes. Let the trumpets blare and the drums roll, because the battle was on.

He began with calm reasoning, presented in a pleasant manner. "Mom, the Higher Humanity Institute could really improve my education."

She fiercely chopped celery. "You're not going."

"Because?"

"Because I think there's something wrong with that place. I smell a rat."

"What's that mean?"

She set down her knife with a thunk. "It *means* it could be dangerous."

He had to suck in a breath at that one and remind himself to stay reasonable. "But what about the other kids, like Rachel? They wouldn't be there if—"

"Who's Rachel?"

"Mrs. Prouse's granddaughter." (He'd read the letter eight times by now.)

"Don't you know bait when you see it?"

It was time for a different angle. "Couldn't I try it for, like, a day or two?"

"No."

"Asiel will be with me. You let me fly all the way to Minneapolis with him."

"I felt good about that. I don't feel at all good about this."

"But what could happen in just a—"

"No!"

So much for logic.

Next tactic: bribery. He tried it in the car on the way to the grocery store. "How 'bout I do the laundry and dishes for a whole month?"

"No."

"Shampoo the rugs?"

"*No.*"

Okay; next tactic.

Only now, he was getting desperate enough to whine. They were at it again in the front room after supper that evening. "You won't let me be in sports 'cause we can't afford it. This won't cost anything. Please, Mom?"

At least he made her answer more gently. "I'm sorry, Hon, but no. How many times do I have to say it? I sense—"

"You sense danger in everything! Ooh, don't try that new toothpaste. It could cause cancer!"

He stalked to his room, slamming the door to make his point. Mom followed and what happened next was a verbal brawl that started in his room until Mom turned on her heel and left, with him hot after her. Dana, playing Barbies on the couch, rolled her eyes.

"I hate that school!" he yelled at Mom's back as they entered the front room. "Sid and the Big Butt Gang have got it in for me! And you don't even care!"

She rounded on him. "Oh, yes I do, and you know it!"

"Then let me get away from them. Let me be with other kids like me."

That shook her. Still, she was stubborn. "No."

"Fine, then! I can just stay and keep getting the stuffing beat out of me!"

"You are not going!"

The phone rang, putting an instant end to the shouting. It was Mrs. Junge, asking if everything was all right.

No more trying to win. He simply had to take action. Mom was being ridiculous. Dad would've understood and would've let him go, and it was time to take matters into his own hands. He stuffed clothes into his Spiderman pack with the one strap still hanging loose, crammed extra socks in his jacket pockets, and snuck out to the balcony.

He would've gone invisible if he could've made the pack do the same. But Asiel had spoken the truth, as if he'd do anything else. Nothing that he carried from the earthly, living realm either disappeared with him or passed through anything.

Snow fell thickly that day. The balcony had a treacherous coating of ice on it under six inches of fluffy snow. He held onto the rail, fighting off his second thoughts, working up the courage to leave.

Mom must've spotted him from the front room. The next thing he knew, she shoved open the sliding door. "What do you think you're doing?" she barked.

"Flying there."

"Don't be stupid! Get in here!"

He lifted off. She lunged for him, but she was wearing only tennis shoes with her jeans and sweatshirt. She managed to catch hold of his jacket, and her feet slid out from under her. She gave one shriek, as sharp and brief as a whip crack. He spun and caught her, barely keeping her head from smashing through the window. He landed and righted her.

They were eye-to-eye, both furious. "If they do something terrible to you," she snarled, "it's your own fault!"

He burst into a grin and hugged her.

Chapter 6

HIGHER HUMANITY

A STAFF PERSON at the Higher Humanity Institute had booked an 8:00 AM. flight for them. Grandma Jean, driving them to the Minneapolis airport, picked them up at 5:30. The parking lot was deserted.

Jeremy hoisted the suitcases into the back of her minivan. "The reporters must be in bed," he said to Dana. "They'll miss us leaving. Too bad. So sad."

They both laughed.

Jeremy hadn't been awake this early in years. It was still dark out, except the sky looked lighter gray toward the east.

Grandma drove fast. They made it to downtown Minneapolis in only forty minutes, passing skyscrapers and the Humphrey Dome stadium as fast as flying. She'd told them not to bother eating breakfast because she'd treat them. They ate in an airport food court. Jeremy ordered a sausage-and-egg biscuit, hash browns, and orange juice.

Grandma had a thick waist and Mom's brown hair, slightly lighter in shade because she colored it. She kept it short and curly, and she liked to wear jeans and sweaters with birds and flowers on them. They sat at a small round table surrounded by early travelers looking as tired as Mom did. Dana was chatty, telling Grandma about school and her friends. Jeremy chomped down his last hash brown patty, too wound up to talk much.

Mom had filled Grandma in on Jeremy's newfound gifts. She wanted to ask him questions now that she had him face to face and didn't have to concentrate on driving. He could see it in her bright eyes. "So, this school …" she ventured, keeping her voice down.

"For kids who can fly," he said, point blank.

She coughed and grew teary eyed, and it was a good thing she'd finished her last swallow of coffee.

The ticket takers called them to board. Grandma hurried after them for a last set of kisses and hugs. "You want me to prove how strong I am?" he whispered. "Don't yell." And he lifted her by the waist until her feet were even with his stomach. He held her aloft for the count of ten, but people started to notice. He set her down easily. She laughed and laughed, keeping it soft, shaking her head.

She gave Jeremy a longer hug than usual and then left them, still chuckling, remarking to a staring executive, "My grandson's a weight lifter."

The man frowned, completely skeptical. "Doesn't look it."

"Show off," said Dana.

They boarded the plane at 7:40, the eastern sky red from the sunrise. Jeremy had crammed a lot of stuff into a small, carry-on suitcase he'd borrowed from Grandma. Mom limited the size of his check-in suitcase. The HHI didn't cover the luggage fee.

He and Dana had flown in a jet only once before, back when Mom and Dad were together, and they'd taken Dana and him to Disneyland®. After the four-and-a half hour flight to Los Angeles, he'd been ready to climb across the seat backs. This time, he cheerfully read, snacked on peanuts, and listened to music on the airplane radio channels with a rental headphone.

He wouldn't have to face Sid and company again. He'd beat the reporters. It all made him want to laugh.

Around 9:30, he felt the jet angle gently and begin its gradual descent. He could see the ground easily through the clean air. Mom made him give Dana the window seat, but he leaned past her head to stare at the black stretches of woodland cut by silver rivers and lakes or the golden-brown fields. It hadn't snowed in Missouri.

The plane dipped. Dana gave a soft giggle from the stomach surge it gave her. They'd dropped quite a bit, by now. He could see thread-thin roads and the wider bands of an interstate.

"Ladies and gentlemen, we'll be landing at Kansas City International Airport in twenty minutes to clear skies," said the pilot over the intercom. "It's sunny and a mild fifty-six degrees. We ask, at this time, that you return to your seats and fasten your seatbelts."

The ground drew nearer. Specks of vehicles flowed along the interlacing highways below. The pilot told the flight attendants to sit. They were over the northern suburbs now. The neighborhoods were laid out in squares and tightly lined with houses, their driveways perpendicular to the streets. They looked like computer chips from up here. He also saw boxy warehouses.

Sun flashed off the wide, brown river with bridges spanning it. "The Mississippi!" sang out Dana who proceeded to spell it in rhythm.

"No, it's the Missouri," he countered.

She spelled that, too. She was the best speller in her class.

They circled at the height he flew on his own. That was a weird thought! If something happened to the plane, he could jump out any old time, and he was strong enough to carry Mom and Dana with him.

The plane stopped its circling for the straight descent to the runway. The ground passed under them very fast. Now they were level with trees and buildings, whipping past the windows in a blur. The landing strip was in view.

"Sit back," snapped Mom.

She hated landings.

The Higher Humanity Institute had a driver waiting for them. He had a bushy band of silver hair circling his bald top, and he wore the same tidy, khaki Dickies work pants and shirt that Grandpa often wore. He introduced himself as Henry. He led them to the luggage carousels for Jeremy to retrieve his suitcase.

Henry had a wheeled cart with him, and he strapped Jeremy's luggage to it, busy and whistling. Mom could hardly suspect him of anything, could she?

"Well, it's ten-thirty," he said. "If you can stand the wait, you'll be at the Institute around noon and you can lunch there. You're gonna love the food."

Henry winked at him. Somehow, Jeremy didn't mind being winked at by a universal grandpa like him. He met them at the airport pickup area in a dark blue van with the Higher Humanity Institute logo and name in yellow on the side panel. Jeremy and Dana sat on the van's first bench; Mom had the front passenger seat.

He drove smoothly through stop-and-go traffic that would've made Mom a nervous wreck. Just as Jeremy was getting restless, they merged onto Highway 71 and left the suburbs for woods and farmland.

"Too bad you missed the fall colors," Henry said. "Lotsa maples and sweet gum 'round here. Reds like you wouldn't believe."

Mom seemed to be relaxing a little, in spite of herself. "Have you lived in Missouri all your life, Henry?"

Yes, he had. The grownups chatted about what the winters were like in Missouri. Jeremy fidgeted, sorely missing his iPod. He already knew the Higher Humanity Institute was a good place. He kept seeing Rachel in his mind and wondered if she'd be there and if he'd meet her. His palms dampened. He'd worn his best jeans and an in-fashion sweatshirt, just in case. His messy curls were close enough to the bed-head look without him having to work at it.

They arrived a few minutes after noon, Henry telling them all about the Institute as they followed the driveway winding through thick woods. "It was a teacher's school—one of the best in the country, but it's too far off the beaten path to stay open, especially with the state universities kids can pick now."

The forest opened up to a long campus running along the shoreline of Lake of the Ozarks. Jeremy hopped out of the van, grinning.

The buildings looked old and interesting, made of red brick with vines growing on their walls. The broad steps and tall front columns were white, the posts wrapped in Christmas lights. Marigolds, blighted by frost, still had a little color to them, and the grass was green. This was definitely not Minnesota in December!

He saw full-grown maples and oaks everywhere, as though the college founders had wished to save every tree they could. The lake, some three hundred yards away, sparkled through their trunks.

Dana cried out, loving it. Jeremy kept quiet, out of caution. Mom still had the power to change her mind and drag him home again.

Asphalt walking paths wound through the woods with white, wrought-iron benches to sit on. The two large, square-shaped, three-story buildings stood at a right angle to each other, and a rectangular two-story to the rear had several garage doors, each with its own little driveway.

A closely mowed open space to the west of the buildings looked like an athletics field, but it didn't have goal posts, soccer nets, or a running track, at least not one that he could see from here. Instead, he saw dozens of tall posts in two long lines, one set painted red and the other blue, with matching banners. Intriguing!

This place beat Anoka Middle School into the dust.

He helped Henry hoist the luggage onto a wheeled cart. Henry led them to the first of the three-story buildings. A white sign, carved with curves and points that Mom called "Colonial style" stood beside the entrance walk. It said "Fletcher Dormitory" in old-English lettering. Henry towed the cart up the handicapped ramp to the side of the steps, and he wouldn't let Jeremy help. He waited out front with Mom and Dana.

Sharp, clacking footsteps coming from the second building made them look. One of the largest women Jeremy had ever seen marched toward them, her heels tapping the asphalt harshly. She was tall, broad-shouldered, and stout at the waist. Her calves that showed under her knee-length skirt looked as large as a football player's legs. She should have had gray hair, judging by her wrinkles, but she'd colored it yellow and wore it in a braided bun. She had on a very brown suit-and-skirt, and a chain dangled on the bow of her glasses. Her face was large-boned and caked with makeup, her lashes so thick they looked fake. Scary!

He guessed she was around Grandma's age, seventy-five, only the two women couldn't have been more different. If Grandma could be likened to a bunny rabbit, then this lady was a grizzly bear.

She came straight at them, reaching out her hand. "Mrs. Lapoint?" the lady boomed. Mom reached back, gingerly. Her handshake looked like it hurt.

"Jeremy?" He winced at the grip of her manly hand.

"And Dana." She didn't seem to spare any strength on her, either. Dana's eyes bugged out at the clasp, but she had the sense to keep quiet and hide her hand behind her back as she shook the circulation back into it.

"Welcome. I'm Louisa Prouse, Director of the Higher Humanity Institute. Henry will show you our campus after your lunch. We all live and dine in Fletcher Dorm, you know. Classes are next door in Walker Hall. This was the John H. Walker Teacher's School when it was built in 1883."

"It's lovely," put in Mom, shakily.

Prouse hurried on, her heels drumming on the walk.

Henry stood on the Fletcher Dorm porch, chuckling. "Don't let her scare you."

"Is she a teacher, too?" asked Jeremy.

"Only one subject. Human studies, her pet thing. Behave yourself and you won't see too much of her."

"I'll behave myself," he promised fervently.

Fletcher Dorm hadn't changed much in a hundred-twenty years. The wooden wall panels in the foyer looked older than the trees outside. Henry kept the speckled granite floor polished and its varnished windowsills, wide enough to sit on, had worn patches from all the students who had plunked their bottoms on them, choosing them for a chatting place over the chairs in their floor lounges. The wooden stair banisters looked as big around as tree trunks with sturdy square balustrades on their ends. Jeremy wanted to straddle them and slide.

After letting them admire the foyer, Henry briefly showed them to the second-floor dorm room Jeremy would share with two other seventh grade boys. They left his things there and hurried to the dining room, which they had to themselves for lunch. The other students were in class.

The dining room was no cold institutional cafeteria either. It had round tables covered with linen cloths, poinsettias for centerpieces, and looked more like a hotel restaurant. Nature art hung on the walls, painted in warm earth tones of beige and rust-red. Large, modern picture windows provided a good view of the lake.

The cook's assistant was a chatty, efficient African-American lady named Mona with hair just turning gray, who served them taco meat in a covered dish, hot and fresh, along with warm, crispy taco shells with plenty of tomatoes, lettuce, cheese, and sour cream. There was also a dish of Spanish rice on the side. She also brought them milk and juice, coffee for Mom, and chocolate chip cookies for dessert.

Henry had not exaggerated. The food was great. Still, Jeremy was disappointed by having to eat with just his family … until one of his tacos broke in half and spilled in his lap. That made him glad Rachel wasn't there to see it.

After lunch, Henry brought them into Walker Hall and up the stairs. They held classes on the second floor, he explained. He showed them the room for human studies, empty now, paneled and floored with the same gold-toned wood that Jeremy saw all over the place. The heavy-paned windows looked too old to open. Silver radiators stood under them; the antique kind that resembled pipes with fancy designs on them, squished together like a fat accordion. Mom frowned.

"Those are just for show," Henry explained. He was very observant. "We put in central heating, all new. Brand new desks. Brand new computers. Best of everything,"

Mom merely gave him a nod. Jeremy's heart tightened. She wasn't convinced yet.

They visited the nurse's office on the third floor. Mom filled out registration and health forms until he was restless enough to want to fly out the windows. Dana was so bored she tried to read a health pamphlet about the importance of hand washing. She asked Jeremy what the word "influenza" meant.

"Mexican pig flu," he told her, off the top of his head. "It makes you throw up tacos."

"Does not." She went on reading, frowning in disgust.

When would he meet his classmates?

At last, Henry led them outside for a tour of the grounds. An asphalt path through the woods led them to the lakefront with a short beach and a swimming dock. "The lake'll feel good for swimming from May on," Henry explained.

Jeremy liked to swim. Dana moaned with envy. And Mom … smiled!

Henry led them along the path to the Athletics Field. Young voices carried through the trees, shouting and shrieking. Jeremy's hands moistened again.

CHILDREN OF ANGELS

The twenty-nine students enrolled at the Higher Humanity Institute stood in two lines at the near end of the field, their backs to him, each team facing its set of posts—the red or the blue. Mom and Dana cried out in amazement at what they were doing. Jeremy drew breath at whom he saw.

The teens were caught up in a flying relay race. Near the front of her line, urging her teammates on, stood Rachel. Her toffee-colored hair was in a ponytail. She looked wonderful in the dark blue HHI shirt and sweat pants that all the students wore, with bright yellow letters, a logo, and stripe running down the side of each leg.

One teen flew the red course against another, racing the blue. They soared a hundred feet above the ground—fast. That is, until they reached the line of bannered posts. Then they controlled their speed enough to zigzag through the course. Now that Jeremy stood end-on to the lines, he could see the posts' irregular zigzags.

It was like the slalom ski races he loved to watch in the Olympics … only the competitors passed each post lengthwise, not up-and-down, as a ski racer did. They took each post on the correct side, by the look of it. They arced right, left, right, left … as fast as they could … fast enough to beat the other team's flyer.

Once each racer passed the zigzagged posts, he or she sped to the yellow pole at the end of his or her course and whapped the huge lollipop-looking circle at the top, making it spin, blurring the red whorl on white. Then they flew around each end post and straight back to the starting lines, pushing with all their speed. The next flyer for each team stood poised, ready to launch.

Sweet! Jeremy usually hated phys-ed, but this drill looked fun.

A lanky man supervised the race, dressed in an HHI shirt and baggy shorts, his legs long and wire-lean, making Jeremy think of a heron.

The next two flyers took off, almost neck-and-neck, a girl against a boy, both of them Jeremy's age. The boy, short and scrawny with a dark complexion and jet-black hair, flew ahead, but not by much. The African-American girl, chunky at the waist, muscled in the legs, wore her hair in a wild ponytail. She clenched her fists, fighting to gain on him.

They wove through the zigzag courses, the boy gaining. But once the girl cleared the slalom section, she poured on the coals! They reached the swirl-striped targets nearly together. The boy slapped his. It spun hard. He made a tight turn around the back of the target post.

The girl missed her target and had to hover, pawing at it. She made it spin, but she'd lost her momentum. She rounded the post and fought to pick up speed. Only now, she was a quarter of the field behind her competition. She squeezed her fists and burned home at the top of her speed.

The boy's head start held. A striped bar between two posts marked the end of each course. He grabbed his blue-striped bar first, of course, and flipped around it like a gymnast, whooping. His team cheered, and the girl at the head of the blue team took off.

The African-American girl reached her red-striped bar a long second later and dropped straight down, mad at herself. The red team's flyer launched out.

Rachel was next, but she didn't brace herself to go. Instead, she did something that shocked Jeremy to his shoes. She turned, gave him a smile, and *beckoned him over.*

He walked in a near daze, hoping he wouldn't trip over anything.

"Hi. Jeremy? I'm Rachel."

"Yeah," he stammered. "I mean, hi."

It was enough of a blunder to make him want to go invisible right there. She didn't seem to notice. She plopped her hand on the African-American girl's shoulder. "And this is Tameeka."

"An' get ready!" Tameeka ordered her.

"Oh!" Rachel faced front with a gasp. The blue team's flyer had just reached her bar, with Rachel's teammate a third of the field behind.

Tameeka turned her intensity on Jeremy. "Join us, hey! We short a flyer. Go, Rachel!"

Rachel's teammate grabbed the red-striped bar. She took off with a shriek. Jeremy planted himself in her place at the head of the line as Tameeka poured instructions in his ear. "Go to the left of the first post. You see that? Then right. An' don't miss any! They set 'em all over the place."

Rachel darted through the slalom portion as quick as a fish.

"She's fast!" he said to Tameeka.

"That's why she always last in the relays. To make up time for dummies like me that louse it up. And then our first flyer, Eric, he has to go again. He fast, too. Except now, you here."

Would he be fast compared to the others or just another loser like he was at everything else?

Rachel's competitor, an older teen, had great speed and a good lead. Rachel couldn't catch her, though she made a perfect hit on her target and a good turn around the target post. She raced home as fast as a falcon.

The blue team's last flyer, waiting to go with his muscles steeled, sized Jeremy up. He looked impossible to beat. He had the same complexion as the boy who'd beaten Tameeka. He was sixteen, maybe, and wore his long black hair in a braid. The tattoos on his tight-muscled arms and chest were nothing short of scary: bats with knives in their claws and snakes curling around daggers. He looked like he belonged in a street gang.

His keen, rust-brown eyes gave off a tiger's hunger and power. He scanned Jeremy up and down, full of scorn.

Why couldn't he fly against a wispy twelve-year-old girl?

The blue team flyer reached her bar, and Tiger Guy took off. Jeremy tightened his muscles for the launch.

69

"Don't miss the last slalom post, either." Tameeka coached him. "It's way outta line. You gotta look for it."

Rachel reached the red-striped bar. He sprang in the air, thrust out his arms, and raced out, the Tiger Guy half the field ahead of him. Jeremy raced to the red posts, *shoom!* But then he had to slow way down. He arced left of the first one, staying close. Now the right. Way wide! He angled back toward the next, angry. He bumped it with his shoulder, setting it rocking. It stung. He shot toward the right. Whoa! It was closer than it looked. He had to cut hard.

He felt as slow as a slug. He fought left, right, left, right … last one! He shot past it and straightened, sped up. No! He'd missed the last post. Tameeka had warned him. It was way off to the right.

"Go back!" she shrieked in the distance.

He doubled back as fast as a diving hawk, arced around the last post, and shot toward the target. He was really mad now.

He hit the target with a grunt. It spun like it was caught in a hurricane. He made a quick turn around the post. Only now, Tiger Guy was two-thirds of the field ahead of him, smoking home. Jeremy set his teeth. He clamped his arms to his ears as Asiel taught him, felt the power build, and went incandescent!

He surged ahead like a jet on thrusters, passing Tiger Guy. The red-striped bar came at him in a blink. He slowed at once, grabbed it, and flipped around, his body outstretched, though he'd never done such a thing before. He landed, laughing.

The others stood staring at him, no one making a sound. He shut his mouth so hard his teeth clicked. He was still sunburst bright. He dimmed immediately.

The stone silence would've made the blood rush to his face if he hadn't been hot from the hard work. His face throbbed so hard he must have looked purple.

Tiger Guy caught his bar and dropped quietly, setting his surly glare on him. The others stared at him as if he were demonic.

"What!" he blurted out. "You can all do this."

Dana had the courage to break the silence with clapping, she was so proud of him. Mom beamed. The others clapped a little.

The teacher hastened to the rescue. "Everyone, this is Jeremy Lapoint from Minnesota. I'm Mr. Bock. Welcome to the HHI. Can you show them?"

Jeremy gave a shrug.

"I'll try," piped up Tameeka. "What do I do?"

"You just have to want to go bright."

She dropped her eyes, concentrating. The silence grew louder. Nothing happened. She raised her face to him, grimacing. His heart sank.

Tiger Guy gave him a curt nod. "You think I can do it, Jet Man?" He shut his eyes. Jeremy watched his arm muscles firm into wires. He formed fists.

Once more, nothing happened. He opened his eyes, still scornful.

"Or not," said Jeremy lamely.

His dorm room felt antique, old, and interesting, with carved wood trim, tan-painted walls, and curtains that looked like one of Grandma's lacy table doilies. "Crocheted curtains," Mom said, sounding impressed for the first time.

His roommates were here, regarding him keenly. They had racecar and sports posters plastered on the walls above their beds. He'd brought a few posters of his own of superhero movies scenes. Mom and Dana put them up for him while Mom made small talk.

"I'm Josh Bergren, and I'm from the Twin Cities, too," the first boy said, in answer to Mom's question. He had sandy hair and freckles. "I live in Plymouth. Hey, we could fly to each others' houses."

Was he really this friendly or was he putting on a show in front of Mom?

Jeremy's second roommate, the Hispanic boy who had beaten Tameeka in the flying relays, took up the talk. "I'm Epifano Ruiz. But call me Epi. I'm from East Los Angeles."

Mom kept it up. Jeremy listened with half an ear to Epi's description of Los Angeles while he took in more details: the wood floor had the same shine that he saw on all the floors at the Institute. Some of the slats had pulled apart from each other over time, but the varnish was thick enough to fill in the gaps. A huge, oval, braided rug colored cream and chocolate brown covered the space between the beds, one against one wall and two opposite. He had the bed nearest the door on the two-bed side.

The quilted bedspreads on the twin beds were brown, too. His own computer and study desk sat against the wall beside the head of his bed. He had his own chest of drawers and a third of the closet waiting to be filled. Not bad!

He made short work of putting away his stuff, then took to studying his roommates, taking care not to be obvious about it.

Epi looked like the Tiger Guy, with the same bronze complexion and rust-colored eyes. However, he wore his straight, blue-black hair short, and he wasn't one bit scary. No tattoos, yet. He must've been TG's younger brother. If so, Jeremy wondered how he had managed to live so long.

He looked out the window. The HHI van pulled alongside the dorm, and Henry climbed out. He'd take Mom and Dana back to Kansas City Airport for their evening flight home.

Jeremy followed them to the van. He never expected to feel lonely as he gave Mom and Dana good-bye hugs. But loneliness was here, taking color out of the world the way the growing dusk turned the evening gray as the sun sank behind the trees to the west.

Mom noticed. "You don't have to stay."

He backed away a step. She sighed, hugged him, and gave him a kiss on the face. Dana hugged him in her light, shy way and climbed in to the bench seat. Mom took her place in front. Henry slammed the doors shut, clouted him on the shoulder as his way of saying, "You'll be fine," and started the van.

Dana waved out the side window until they were out of sight.

Jeremy turned away, dragging his feet. The sun had set now, setting the western end of the lake on fire with its reflection. Shadows grew into darkness. He caught a movement in the woods, just a flicker of something with the corner of his eye. Something large and dark was moving in there.

He stopped for a hard look, his heart speeding up. There, something flew from tree to tree, but going so fast he wasn't sure if he really saw it. His eyes must be playing tricks … No! He caught a glimpse of large, bat-like wings. Then the shadow thing was gone.

A demon? Icy fright hit him. "Asiel?" he whispered. "Did you see that?"

"The enemy is always near," said the angel. He didn't appear.

What a great comfort! Maybe Mom had been right to mistrust this place. Jeremy hurried to the dorm.

Jeremy, jumpy now, followed Epi and Josh into the cafeteria where many students and teachers had already gathered. The air buzzed with talk that ebbed just a little as he stepped into the room and then picked up again eagerly. He hated it.

The teachers sat at a long, oval table at the front of the room. Mrs. Prouse's female baritone carried over the other adult voices. She acknowledged Jeremy with a nod but did not smile. He wondered if she ever did.

They made their way to the seventh graders' table. Three girls sat on "their" side. A clear gap in the chairs on each side showed the demarcation line. Jeremy took the chair by Josh.

Rachel smiled at him. He managed a lopsided grin back and bumped over his water glass. It was empty, thank heaven.

Tameeka bustled in, made a beeline for their table, and to Jeremy's mortification, sat beside him, completely ignoring the invisible gender line.

"I got a question for you," she began. "How come you're the only one who can make yourself glow like lightning?"

She could irritate the Pope. "I dunno. Maybe you have to be excited or something."

"Sorry. Didn' mean to make you mad."

Epi was pouring himself a glass of water from a stainless steel pitcher. "My brother's mad. He don't like to lose."

Jeremy had guessed right about them being brothers. "What's his name?"

"Oscar Ruiz. Only you don't wanna call him that. Okay? Call him Sharp."

"Sharp," repeated Jeremy.

"What else can you do?" Tameeka asked him. Was she this blunt about everything?

Josh rose to his rescue. Maybe he was going to be a friend. "Wouldn't you rather talk about clothes?"

That earned him scowls from all four of the girls. Jeremy would've ignored Tameeka's question if Rachel hadn't picked up on it. "Can you do other things, Jeremy?"

What the heck? "I can go through walls," he answered quietly.

The others gaped at him. "I ain't tryin' that," vowed Epi.

Jeremy was still stuck on the puzzle of why he could go bright and the other young Nephilim couldn't. "My angel keeps telling me you can do these things just 'cause you want to."

"Your what?" asked Tameeka, her eyes widening. The others stared too.

"My angel. His name is Asiel."

Epi made the sign of the cross on himself from his forehead to his stomach and across his chest, the way Jeremy had seen Catholics do. "A real live angel? You can, like, see him? You swear to it?"

"He's not visible right now, but, yeah. He's my guardian angel."

And quit looking at me like I'm nuts or a miracle worker, he wanted to add. He escaped their eyes by looking out the picture window, sort-of taking in the salmon-colored sunset on the lake, fading to coral with faint strips of green and purple on the edge of the night sky.

Whoosh! A huge pterodactyl-thing flew past the windows, its wings outspread for a landing. It passed in and out of sight so fast that Jeremy had no time to yell for the others to look. He gulped and took a quick inventory: no one else had seen it. He decided to keep quiet. But, man! Was this place infested with demons or what?

Mona came in wheeling a large, stainless steel cart loaded with covered metal platters and serving bowls. "Roast chicken tonight, folks," she announced. "An' whipped potatoes, an' gravy, an' corn, an' coleslaw. An' brownies for dessert!"

The other students applauded. Tameeka returned to the girls' side of the table. Another lady hurried into the room to help Mona place the serving dishes on the tables, quickly and pleasantly.

"Don't tell old Man-Lady Prouse about your guardian," Epi warned Jeremy. "She's not into angels."

"What do you mean?" Jeremy asked him, his voice sharp. He was still shaky over seeing another demon.

The other seventh graders exchanged knowing glances. "You'll see," said Tameeka, ominously.

Chapter 7

ENEMIES

THE WALKER HALL foyer was stony and filled with echoes. A gigantic bronze plaque on the wall facing the entrance said, "To teach is to inspire." Jonathan H. Walker's admirers had immortalized his face in a large bronze cutting under the words. It looked like some wrinkly old man to Jeremy.

The wooden staircase had the same huge, polished banister and railings that the builders had put in Fletcher Dorm. But only someone like Sid Lundahl would be dumb enough to try sliding on them. This was a very serious building.

Jeremy had Prouse for his first class. Mr. Bock, his advisor, gave him his textbooks, and he made his way up the stairs with Epi and Josh and entered the first door on the left. All thirty students took

Human Studies. Jeremy kept himself near Epi and Josh, toward the back. Sharp sat with the older teen boys, quietly joking about something that raised low-pitched laughs as they walked in. He tossed a cold glance at Jeremy. They were laughing at him. He knew it.

Then he saw Rachel sitting near the front, chattering with Tameeka and two other girls in the desks around her. She noticed Jeremy and astounded him, once again, with a wave and a smile. He sat dreamily, his mood lifted by several notches.

The buzz in the room fell quiet at the sound of clacking footsteps. Louisa Prouse marched in the room, her suit and skirt gray. She placed notes on the podium at the front of the class and gave out a crisp, "Good morning, class." Thank goodness she didn't make them answer her back in chorus!

Her voice filled the room. "Your assignment was the question, 'What are the Responsibilities of Being a Higher Form of Human?' Before I collect your answers, would anyone read theirs?"

She glowered at them through a fidgety silence. Finally, an older teen girl raised her hand. She had flat brown hair, small eyes, thick cheeks, and pouty lips.

"Melissa," Josh whispered to him and grimaced.

Melissa read in monotone, her voice reedy-sounding. "The responsibilities of being a Higher Human are: We must be kind. We must use our powers to help people. We shouldn't hurt anyone."

And that was that.

"Barely adequate!" thundered Prouse. "Remember, youngsters, you are the first to reach the next level of Human Development. You have climbed the rung. That's why you can fly."

That shook Jeremy. He blinked hard, and his heart thumped.

"That's why you are stronger, at your tender age, than a grown man. You are the privileged few, and in a short time, I plan to astound the world with what you are."

Against his better judgment and will, Jeremy shook his head. He couldn't help himself, and she saw him! "Young man?"

"Mrs. Prouse," he faltered. "We're Nephilim."

Her hand bumped the podium. Her lecture notes dropped and scattered across the floor. Rachel and several other girls hopped up to gather them. Prouse ignored them, her eyes boring in on Jeremy. "Where did you learn that word?"

"It's … we're in the Bible, Genesis, Chapter Six. We are part angel."

The other students reacted with short cries of amazement or scorn. Epi, Josh, and Tameeka shot him looks, ordering him to shut up. Now.

The girls gave the sheets they'd picked up to Rachel, who, as the Man-Lady's granddaughter, had the privilege of setting them on the podium before hurrying back to her desk.

Prouse, it seemed, had been collecting her thoughts and her breath. "You are referring to the legend that was incorporated into the creation myth by ancient races in their ignorance, explaining nature through mysticism."

Jeremy hardly understood a word she said. She took a moment to rearrange her pages. He saw a slight tremble in her hands. "There are no such things as angels or half-angels. You may as well believe in fairies, elves, and goblins while you're at it."

That drew a brief laugh from the class.

"Now, then! Open your books to page eighty-three, chapter four, 'Know Your Genetics.'"

The students obeyed with the slapping of book covers and the rustling of pages.

"And young man," added Prouse, eyeing Jeremy, "see me in my office after lunch."

Epi, Josh, and Tameeka cringed on his behalf, as if he wasn't dreading it enough.

His other classes weren't so bad, since he had no other classes with the whole of HHI except phys-ed, the last subject of the day. He walked across the hall to seventh and eighth grade math. For basic subjects like math, English, and science, seventh and eighth graders were together in one class while ninth and tenth graders were in the other. No student over sixteen attended the school. Did that mean there were no new Nephilim older than that in the world?

Jeremy felt certain that Prouse would have brought them here if they existed. Mom's suspicions grew in him. Did the Man-Lady have a dark agenda? Why did she drive like a tank over anyone who believed in angels? And why did the HHI have demons all over the place?

He tried to concentrate on his new schoolwork. The math teacher, a pleasant woman in her early thirties named Mrs. Harrisburg, managed to make percentages interesting. He had science next, in a lab with shiny Formica counters over old cupboards and brand new equipment. Interesting animals scratched or napped in their cages: white rats almost as large as cats, field mice, and a chameleon named Seymour.

Mr. Bock taught all science classes. He spoke with a flat voice and deadpan face, but Jeremy listened because he liked the subject. Today's lecture was on plant parts, something he already knew. Bock had them cut daisies to smithereens.

"Wait 'til we do the same thing to dead worms," said Josh with yellow pollen stuck to his face, adding to his freckles.

"Done that," said Jeremy.

The whole school ate lunch together. He sat in his chair near the window, facing the lake, hardly daring to look … and saw only a squirrel dart from one tree to the next. He dreaded what he might face after this. Still, he was hungry. Mona set covered bowls around the poinsettia on the seventh graders' table. Heavenly smells seeped from them, making him hope for one of his favorite meals for a distraction.

She removed the covers with a flourish. Yes! Spaghetti and meatballs in red sauce, salad, and fresh-baked breadsticks.

He dug in. Prouse could yell at him 'til she turned purple if she wanted to; he was going to enjoy this. He sucked in a huge mouthful of strands—no one bothered to wind it around their forks—just as the seventh grade girls came in. Rachel gave him a smile. He was so entranced he let a saucy string slide off his fork. It landed on his shirt, front and center. Seething, he picked it off and wiped the splotch with his napkin.

She didn't sit down in her usual chair. She came over to his chair! He dropped the napkin. Epi and Josh attended busily to their eating. The other girls sat and dished up.

Rachel stood at his shoulder. "I'm sorry Grandma was so hard on you," she said, soft-toned. "She's nervous because she's asked a bunch of TV News channels to come and film us—CNN, Fox, the networks. Isn't that exciting?"

"Yeah. It's … wow," said Jeremy.

She moved to her seat. He cursed himself for not having learned to speak English yet.

Mrs. Prouse marched in and took her place at the teachers' table, accepting Mona's glass of lemonade with a curt smile. She did smile! Then she noticed Jeremy and scowled.

Rachel met his eyes with sympathy, warming him through.

Josh leaned to him, whispering and barely moving his lips. "Hey, I think she likes you."

No way! No girl had ever liked him before, especially one this cute. The prospect of a lecture from Prouse looked less terrible by the second.

Epi frowned toward the empty chair beside an African-American tenth grader named Carl. Sharp was late for lunch. "He loves Italian food," he muttered.

Sharp, as scary as ever, sauntered in the room a few seconds later, as if in answer. He made his way to his chair, but he was nothing compared to what lurched in at his heels.

A gorilla-sized demon followed him in and took a stand by Sharp's table. Its arms and legs were thick and muscled under scaly, gray-green hide. It had a stub-nosed face and black eyes, like a cross between a pig and an ape, if apes had pointed teeth. Its talons, at the end of thick, knobby fingers, were long and curved.

It held an iron shield and wore a black tunic and painful-looking weapons at its belt—a sword in a black scabbard, a pointed dagger, and a spiked chain looped at his side like a monster cowboy's lasso.

Jeremy stood with a cry, knocking over his chair. *Thunk*!

All talk died in an instant. Jeremy, too frightened to think straight, blurted out the first thing that popped in his head. "Epi! Your brother is demon possessed!"

Epi's mouth dropped open in shock. Sharp gave a snort. Carl and the tenth grader next to him broke out in laughter.

"What'd you say I am, *niño loco?*" asked Sharp, full of his trademark scorn.

The demon also glared at Jeremy. "Why can you see me?" it demanded in a horribly guttural voice, like an alligator, if alligators could talk. "One of those sensitive brats, are you?"

It narrowed its eyes, studying the boy. "No. You're a ..."

With a roar, it unsheathed its iron sword and lunged at Jeremy. He leaped sideways, gasping, and the blade missed him by an inch.

Asiel appeared and parried the thrust, his sword silver bright against black iron. *Clack!* The two spirit beings went at it, their blades a blur of light and dark, ringing and clanking like hammers on steel.

Electric bolts shot off Asiel's sword and seared against the demon's dark shield, the sparks burning the creature. It snarled and doubled its attack.

It pushed Asiel back. Jeremy dodged aside or they would've bowled him over. He slammed into the girls' side of the eighth graders' table. Their glasses tipped. Their silverware fell. Melissa's plate of spaghetti dumped on her lap. The eighth graders, all seven of them, scattered, yelling.

Mr. Bock and Mrs. Prouse rose to their feet. "What's wrong, Jeremy?" Bock asked him.

Jeremy froze, aghast. "Can't any of you see? They're fighting!"

All the others looked clean through the combatants, not seeing them at all, but sharing a clear message that this new kid had serious problems. This was more than Jeremy could take. He, alone, saw spirit beings? This was so not fair!

The fight raged on. Asiel leaped in the air to drive down toward his enemy. The demon jumped and met him, their swords bashing together. They fought in mid-air, their wings beating like battling eagles armed with swords.

Asiel zapped his enemy once more. The thing flipped backwards with a grunt, and landed heavily on knobby feet, its shield high. Asiel also landed. The demon panted like a spent dog. They were at a standoff.

"Name yourself," Asiel ordered it.

"Scrag. I command hundreds."

"Dozens, more like."

That drew a hiss from Scrag. Meanwhile, Prouse took command of her protégés, ordering them to be quiet and sit. The eighth graders obeyed her, distracted. Melissa stood by her chair, wiping furiously at her jeans with wet napkins.

Mr. Bock spoke up. "What's frightening you, son? We have a type of tarantula here in Missouri. Is it large and hairy?"

"It's large, yeah," said Jeremy, gasping.

"Mr. Bock, he said they're fighting," Melissa reminded him.

Many of the teens were laughing, by now, Sharp among them. "You lose a couple of rats, Mr. Bock?

Escapees? He's growing them big in the lab, man. They could eat a cat. You scared of rats, *niño loco?*"

He formed his teeth into fangs, drawing harder laughs.

Scrag's laughter sounded like steam escaping from a pipe. Suddenly, he sheathed his sword, raised a claw, and edged toward Rachel, leering.

"No!" Jeremy cried, lunging to put himself between her and Scrag. Asiel clapped a hand to his chest, stopping him in his tracks, and then leaped in front of Rachel, his shield raised. He and Scrag drew their weapons and went at it again, the blades ringing.

"You don't have to yell about it," said Carl.

Prouse raised her voice. "Mona, come here, please, at once."

The room quieted. Mona bustled in through the kitchen door and stopped, surprised to see two students standing, agitated, one of them with her jeans plastered with sauce. "Oh, my, my," she said. "What happened here?"

"Would you be so good as to bring my lunch to my office?"

Mona did her job without getting an answer to her question. She moved smoothly to a side cupboard and removed a tray. She passed a few feet from the still-fighting combatants. Asiel shoved Scrag with his shield. The demon stumbled back, passing clean through Mona.

She stopped, a frown crossing her face. "Somebody open a window? It's chilly all of a sudden."

"Jeremy and Mr. Bock, come with me," commanded Prouse, leaving with the usual clatter of heels.

Scrag sheathed his sword. Asiel kept his raised, flanking Jeremy, who followed Mr. Bock out the door.

Melissa's clarinet voice, raised in anger, followed him out in the hall. "You're buying me a new pair of jeans, freak!"

Laughter rolled out of the dining room. But it was Scrag standing in the doorway, hissing at his back, that made Jeremy look over his shoulder.

Jeremy hurried to keep up with Mr. Bock on the asphalt path to Walker Hall. Neither had a chance of catching Prouse, marching like a soldier. They whipped through the foyer and up the stairs to her office. Jeremy let Bock lead the way through her door, and hung back.

Asiel had stayed with him the whole time, and Scrag had not. The angel sheathed his sword.

"What do I tell them?" Jeremy whispered urgently.

"The truth, for all it's worth to them."

Asiel went invisible.

If she'd designed her office to intimidate students, she'd done a great job. Books lined the bookshelves in perfect uprightness. The desk, made of some dark wood all carved and polished, looked big enough to play pool on. Diplomas, certificates, and award plaques lined the walls. A large portrait of a white-haired, elderly man in a black suit hung behind Prouse's desk, dominating the room. He didn't look any nicer than she did.

Prouse removed a file folder from a tall, black, four-drawer file cabinet in the back corner and sat in her brown leather desk chair, studying Jeremy's file. He stood at the opposite side of the desk. Bock moved to her shoulder and did his own reading.

Mona breezed in, set the tray with covered dishes in front of Prouse, and went on her way again. She spoke warmly to Jeremy. "You get enough dinner?"

"Me? I'm fine."

That made her pause at the door. "Without dessert? You ain't my son. He'd eat his ice cream if a hurricane was takin' the table."

She left, her soft-soled shoes making hardly a sound. Prouse, eating her salad and breadsticks, motioned for Jeremy to sit in a heavily carved wooden chair that looked like it came from an English castle owned by King Henry VIII.

Mr. Bock remained standing.

"Now, Jeremy." Prouse began. "You will be in no trouble whatsoever as long as you answer honestly. What scared you in the dining room?"

"A demon."

The breadstick broke between her fingers. Bock lost all professionalism and stared at Jeremy as if he was deranged.

Prouse recovered quickly. "There is no such thing. You sensed, I think, an emotional imprint from the past. These buildings are old and full of history."

Emotional imprint! He stifled a laugh. "It was as big as a gorilla and it had claws and fangs," he said.

There was a hiss at the door, and the room went darker. Jeremy turned, wincing. Scrag stood in the doorway. "You wished to see me?" he rasped, grinning.

Mr. Bock needed to loosen his tie, but Prouse seemed unfazed by the presence. What she couldn't see, she didn't seem to feel, either. Asiel appeared, of course, between Jeremy and Scrag, his hand on his sword hilt.

"I don't fault you for the prejudices that have been worked into your thinking," said Prouse. "Demons have been a part of human lore since the dawn of our race."

"Now one's standing in your doorway. My guardian angel is here, too."

Prouse lifted aside the tray and wrote something in Jeremy's file.

"Mr. Bock," Jeremy pressed. "You can feel the monster."

"It's a bit stuffy in here."

That drew a wheezy laugh from Scrag.

"Jeremy," Prouse announced, "I'm setting up an appointment for you for this afternoon. Tell Dr. Steenerson, the school psychologist, everything you've told us."

He was getting angry. "You think I'm nuts."

"We do not use such terms here."

"I don't want to."

She cut off his protests like an army sergeant yelling down a private. "There will be no arguing. You may go and finish your lunch."

He wanted to turn on his heel and stalk out fast to cool his temper, however, Scrag still blocked the door. Asiel drew his sword.

Scrag laughed again. "It would be fun, but you get to keep your wings a little longer."

He stepped back into the hall, his black eyes glowing red in the dimness.

Chapter 8

EXAMINATIONS

ASIEL FLANKED JEREMY along the hallway. "Now do you see why you were not given all the truth about the Nephilim when we first met?"

"What! They're gonna …"

"Softly," cautioned Asiel.

Jeremy swallowed his anger enough to drop his voice. "They're gonna torture me or something?"

"The more that Prouse and her allies think you know, the more of a danger you are to them."

What a comforting thought.

He reached the top of the stairs. A quick movement below caught his eye, and he leaned over the top rail for a better look. Carl and Sharp sailed down the last flight of stairs, half-sliding on the banister to speed their descent, their toes barely touching every third step or so, making their exit fast and silent.

Carl shot a look over his shoulder at the bottom landing and met eyes with Jeremy. He grinned like an ape and nudged Sharp. They laughed quietly and passed out of his view.

Fabulous! They'd listened in on his nice little talk with the Man-Lady. Now the whole school would know that the new kid saw demons.

His afternoon classes wouldn't have been so bad if Melissa hadn't been an eighth grader. She arrived for English, the next subject after lunch, wearing different jeans and complaining that the stain would never come out of the ones that caught the spill. "They were my favorites, too," she declared, fiercely.

Jeremy still smoldered. "Get over it," he muttered, not all that softly.

She wheeled to face him in order to make her insult all the stronger. "I hope you get expelled, Sicko."

The teacher, Mr. Nelson, walked in. Melissa slowly faced the front again. Jeremy hardly heard a word of his lesson on prepositions.

His last class ended at three o'clock. He had half-an-hour before his appointment with Dr. Steenerson. He wasn't about to wait around Walker Hall. He hustled back to Fletcher Dorm. Mona had set out snacks on a serving table in the lobby: fruit slices, whole-wheat crackers and cheese, and juice. He grabbed what he wanted and beat it to his room.

Epi and Josh changed into their gym clothes. He'd have to miss phys-ed today, and he wasn't sure if he was glad or sad. It had been fun to beat Sharp. Tomorrow, maybe.

At three-twenty, he trudged back to Walker Hall. He was climbing the front steps when a light voice lifted his heart like sunshine.

"Jeremy," Rachel called, running over to him. "Aren't you coming to phys-ed?"

Only she could make a gym uniform look fabulous. "We're playing flying basketball," she continued. "It took Mr. Bock a month to figure out safety gear 'cause he was afraid we'd kill ourselves running into each other at a hundred feet up. We have to wear so many pads we look like Transformers. It's fun, though. You'd win for us."

"Oh," he said helplessly.

"But you've gotta have your physical, don't you? That's right. We all did that. I'm so dumb."

"No, you're not!"

There was a short, embarrassing pause. "We've got five minutes," she said. "Could you teach me that going bright thing? I almost felt like I could do it."

"I think you have to be, like, hyper or something."

She gave him a look that would outshine any angel's eyes. "Race ya!" she cried out and launched in the air.

She caught him by surprise. She was at tree height by the time he took off, and she was out to beat him. He pushed himself to his top speed.

He drew level with her, feeling energy building in his core. "Go bright!" he ordered her. "Just 'cause you want to!"

He held off doing it. She closed her eyes for a second … and burst into incandescence! She opened her eyes, took in her hands glowing like white neon, and surged forward, shrieking with laughter.

He went bright and chased her.

They neared a small cloud. She raced behind it with him at her heels. He'd have to give it all he had to beat her! The cloud caught their glow and reflected it to them. From the ground, it must have looked like a cloud with the sun behind it, its edges bright. Grandma called them "clouds with a silver lining."

He'd never had so much fun in his life.

It only lasted five minutes. Just as he passed her, Rachel slowed down, turned, and led them back. A cluster of students with Tameeka, Epi, and Josh in the center stood staring up at them.

Rachel landed, still bright, to applause. "I did it! Jeremy taught me how." They both dimmed, her loyal words making it hard for Jeremy to stop shining.

"What did you say we are?" Tameeka asked him.

Hope rose in him. "Nephilim. We're half human and half angel."

But older students drew near, Melissa included. "I don't see how that's possible," she said in that reedy voice of hers.

Carl and Sharp came up last. "Lapoint! Behind you!" Carl cried out. "A demon!"

Jeremy ignored him, but his light heart grew heavy. Meanwhile, Melissa continued her attack as though Carl hadn't said anything. "There's no scientific proof."

Tameeka rose to his defense, hotly. "What! These two made themselves bright like comets by accident?"

"It's gonna eat you!" screamed Carl. The older boys broke out laughing.

"Going bright is just another one of our new, higher human traits," Melissa argued.

Sharp whapped Carl on the back. "Demons don't eat you. They possess you. Don't you know anything?" He suddenly gagged, showed his teeth, and formed his hands into claws, his voice coming out in a growl. "It's got me-e-e-e!"

Carl leaped away in mock terror.

"You're not drooling enough," said Jeremy, trying to joke but growing angrier by the second. "And you need to file your teeth into points."

Snarling, Sharp lurched toward him. Jeremy stood his ground. The older teen girls shrieked and hopped away, and now they were laughing.

That did it. Jeremy turned on Melissa, blasting her. "Why would I make this up? Huh? You think I like being treated like a mental case?"

"You're going to have to get used to it."

Meanwhile, Sharp managed to make himself drool.

"Ew!" cried the older girls.

Carl formed his fingers into a cross to ward off the demon.

Epi stepped in Sharp's way. "Don't make fun of it, man," he scolded his brother, dead serious.

Jeremy wondered why Scrag hadn't shown up.

Melissa changed the subject; her eyes narrowed on him. "Why aren't you in gym clothes, Lapoint?"

"He's getting his physical," Josh answered.

"Is he seeing Dr. *Steenerson?*"

That brought instant quiet. They were keenly interested, in a mean way. Apparently, the good doctor carried a reputation. Whoever had to see him must be crazy.

A whistle sounded. Mr. Bock stood at the edge of the Athletics Field, glaring at them with his hands on his hips. The others moved on. Epi and Josh hung back.

"Don't worry, Lapoint," Carl called back. "The doc'll give you something that'll make you stop seeing demons." They went on, most of them snickering.

Rachel and Tameeka looked back with sympathy; however, they kept going.

"Don't let 'em get to you," said Epi. "They're like a wolf pack, you know? One starts biting and they all attack."

Jeremy glanced at his watch. "It's three-thirty-five. I gotta go."

Epi and Josh made for the athletics field at a trot. Jeremy dragged his feet up the Walker Hall steps.

Asiel suddenly appeared in front of him. "Take nothing they give you," he said.

Jeremy reached the front doors, muttering. "How was your first day, Jeremy? Oh, fine, Mom. Except for the tranquilizers."

Dr. Steenerson's office, on the third floor, was full of messy paintings and wire sculptures. Jeremy guessed he was sixty because he had deep wrinkles on his face and steel-gray hair tied back in a ponytail. His tie looked like abstract art, the same as his paintings.

He warmly welcomed Jeremy, who wasn't impressed a bit, and placed him in a cushioned chair away from his desk. He sat opposite him in another cushioned chair holding a large yellow notepad on a clipboard.

Steenerson made short work of the basics like, "What does your mom do?" and moved on to the real issue. "How long have you been seeing demons, Jeremy?"

"A week."

"Did you ever see things when you were a child?"

"No." The shorter the answers, the better.

Steenerson wrote on his notepad. "How old were you when your father went to prison?"

"Nine."

"Did that bother you?"

What a dumb question. "Yeah, sure."

More writing. Jeremy heard a familiar hiss at the door. It was the nastiest sound he knew, and it sent icy shivers up his back. He couldn't help but look.

Scrag stood leering. Asiel appeared, as always, standing firm.

"I'll cut you to pieces that they can't put back together angel," Scrag taunted him. "And then the little angel-boy is mine."

That drew a soft moan of fear from Jeremy, his face still turned toward the door.

"Can you tell me what's wrong?" Steenerson asked him, gently.

Scrag grinned wider. "Answer the nice doctor."

"Tell him, Jeremy," said Asiel.

"There's a demon in your doorway."

Steenerson wrote intently.

The fright made Jeremy ornery. The doc wanted the truth, eh? "His name is Scrag."

Steenerson looked up, gaping, his professionalism derailed. He hastily pulled a prescription form from under his notebook on the clipboard. He scrawled something on it, and though he managed to regain the warm-yet-business-like manner in his voice, his hands shook. He also spoke rather fast. "Jeremy, the brain has certain chemical combinations going on inside it. For some people, those chemicals are ... out of whack. I'll be right back with a sample."

He strode to the door and out. Scrag chuckled as he stepped aside for him.

Mrs. Prouse entered the office. "Jeremy, follow me."

He hesitated. What was this all about?

"Go with her," Asiel urged him.

Jeremy rose slowly.

Prouse led him down the hall, to a door on the left at the far end. "In here, please," she said, opening the door part way for him.

He walked in and saw, all in half-a-second, a twin bed with one of those brown bedspreads, a table under the window, and shelves with a few books on them. He was just taking in two other things—a sink and a porta-potty—when the door closed and he heard the lock click.

He ran to the door and tried it, in case it had happened by accident. "Mrs. Prouse?" he called out. But all he heard were those clacking footsteps, muffled by the door, marching away.

Anger burst in him like a firecracker. "Hey! What are you doing? You can't leave me in here!" He thumped the door with his fists, and with his new strength, it should've splintered or crashed open. Instead, it gave back a steely *bang* and held firm. It was made of reinforced steel, painted to look like varnished wood grain.

Seething, he backed from the door, and for the first time, he knew how Dad felt except when Dad entered his prison cell, he *expected* the door to be locked behind him.

In the next second, scorn and laughter replaced his rage as he remembered what he could do. Prouse obviously didn't know all her students' traits. He'd just have to clue her in. Hot with triumph, he rose in the air and glided around the room. Ah! There it was. On the highest shelf, hidden amidst books, he saw a video camera.

"So you can study the specimen," Jeremy said aloud, knowing they'd hear it on the audio recorder. "Well, here's a new angel trait for your research. I'm outta here!"

He turned, laughing, and flew for the outer wall, imagining the shock on Prouse's face when she watched the footage of him flying right through the wall.

Asiel appeared, blocking his exit. Jeremy stopped, displeased, and hovered.

The angel was grinning. "I have the best news! You have been called to be a battle leader."

Jeremy didn't like the sound of that. "I just want to go home."

Asiel wasn't listening. "You wondered why only you can see spirit beings. This is your answer." He landed, Jeremy following suit, curiosity pulling at him.

Asiel led him to the corner alongside the camera, where its field of view couldn't reach. A shimmering oval as tall and wide as a door suddenly appeared in front of Jeremy, swirling with colors. He saw evergreen, granite silver, ocean green, and the powder blue of the sky. Then he saw grass green and whorls of all the different colors that flowers could be. There was the brown of rich dirt and the dazzling white of snow. Next, bands of rainbow hues chased each other in the order of the spectrum—purple, blue, green, yellow, orange, and red, as vivid as stained glass with the sun behind it.

He heard wisps and whispers of bird song, waterfalls, dogs yapping, children laughing, piano music, voices speaking, a thread of rock guitar, a car whooshing by on the highway. The muted sounds swirled like the colors.

"It's a travel-way," said Asiel. "Some are stairways up and down from heaven."

Wonder coursed through Jeremy. *Heaven?* Could he go *there?* Longing to do so shot through him on the heels of amazement, heating his heart and making it leap.

"Of course, the heavenly ways are barred to you while the mortal in you remains."

Asiel could just as well have dumped snow on him. Jeremy felt his face fall right with his heart, and he had the strangest urge to cry. He felt as crushed as an eight-year-old told the trip to Disneyland® was cancelled. But why?

Asiel went on. "This is a doorway from one place on earth to another. Follow."

He stepped into the oval. The colors engulfed him, and he disappeared. Jeremy took a breath and drew to within inches of the swirling surface, wondering if Asiel was going to reach back through and yank him in.

He touched a toe to the moving colors. Instantly, his world changed to an alpine meadow deep with sugar-sparkled snow, the bright sun reflecting strongly off the white. He felt the heat on his face despite the cold. The surrounding trees gave off blue shadows and the sapphire sky had snow-white clouds in it. Mountains ringed the meadow, white from their bases to their tops with dark green pines bristling on their faces.

He cried out in pure astonishment. Asiel could tell him if these were the Alps or the Rockies, but he couldn't get the question out. He came close to fainting again. This was no less of a stunner than flying for the first time.

So, this was how angels got around so fast!

Chapter 9

DECISIONS

JEREMY'S SWEATSHIRT, JEANS, and tennis shoes were no proper outfit for an alpine meadow deep with snow. A cold wind blew down off the mountains. He wrapped his arms around his chest and shivered, still staring around him.

"Will yourself to be dressed as I am," said Asiel.

Jeremy gave him a look-over and concentrated. A long white robe replaced his clothes. It felt soft and thick, like one of Grandma's linen tablecloths. A rope of woven gold circled his waist, and his feet went bare inside a pair of leather sandals that bore no buckle or metalwork of any kind. Cords, strung through side leather pieces and tied across the tops, held the sandals snuggly to his feet.

His teeth should have been chattering and his toes should have been turning blue, yet he no longer felt cold. Instead, his toes felt as warm as if he was standing on a sunny beach. He wriggled them and grinned.

"Where are we?" he ventured to ask.

"Your kind has named this place Glacier National Park."

Jeremy squeaked out a laugh. "What state is this? Like, Colorado?"

"Montana."

"Missouri to Montana in a millisecond! Why didn't I bring my snowboard? I don't own a snowboard, but ..."

"You have not been shown the travel-ways for your amusement."

"Dad used to snowmobile with his buddies in Montana. Big Sky! That's the place. He said you have to learn to zigzag your sled back and forth up the steeps or you'll flip the machine over backwards. That really happened to one of Dad's friends. You know, having his snowmobile go end-over-end?"

Asiel let him chatter away without comment. Concentrating, he peered at the ground beyond his feet. A large, round, hammered gold disk appeared, the sun glinting off its curve, a large red cross emblazoned on it. A bronze bow as thick as a good-sized sapling appeared beside it, the copper-colored metal formed with leaf patterns along its face. Next came a leather quiver full of bronze arrows with white feathers. The bow looked too heavy to pick up, let alone draw.

"He broke his collarbone," faltered Jeremy.

Lastly, a sword with a golden hilt in a burnished leather scabbard and belt appeared.

"H-he could've been killed."

Asiel's eyes were alight. "Gird your sword about you."

"Who would I fight?"

"The demon, Scrag, and his underlings."

Jeremy backed away from the weapons. "Me!? Fight that thing? He'll cut my arms off."

"Why do you build up your fear?"

Asiel waited. Out of sheer obedience, his hands trembling, Jeremy picked up the sword and scabbard, tip downward. The hilt felt cold. The blade weighed as heavy as iron. Without his new strength, he would've had no hope of lifting it.

He fastened the sword belt around him, his hands stiff and clumsy, and cold had nothing to do with it. The sword pulled the belt hard against his opposite hip and bumped his leg.

"How did knights walk with these things on?" he griped.

Asiel drew his sword, *s-s-shing*, and held it tip-up in front of his face. Then he raised it heavenward, one-armed. "The salute to the King of Kings."

Jeremy pulled on the hilt, hoping he'd feel an inflowing of something more than fear as the blade pulled free. Instead, it was all he could do to get it out of its sleeve. The scabbard fit tightly and wanted to go with the sword. He had to hold it firmly with his left hand and pull on the hilt with his right. The blade was so long, the tip wouldn't quite clear the scabbard, even at the end of his reach. He tugged, jiggled, and tugged some more, suddenly realizing he was turning in circles. He stopped, his face hot.

He gave another tremendous tug and the blade came free. The sun caught it. It flashed like a beacon. The edges looked horrifying—hard, gleaming steel honed sharp enough to cut off his ear if he swung the blade too far around. He swallowed hard and grasped the hilt two-handed, waiting for an infilling of power.

He felt only the weight dragging at his arms and shoulders. "The salute," Asiel reminded him.

Jeremy raised the tip, shakily, to about a sixty-degree angle to his chest.

"Your blade should be straight up and down."

"I'll cut my nose off."

He straightened it a little more, then raised it clumsily with both hands, maybe five inches. "Why does it feel so heavy? I thought I was stronger than a man."

"No man could hope to lift that sword. Your arms will find their strength as it is given. You must believe. Now, the strike. It's important to keep the blade narrow to the air, so as not to slow it with dragging. Tilt it as you turn it. Like this." Asiel did a wide, two-handed sweep with his blade, like a homerun hitter swinging his bat, keeping it edge-on, cutting it through the air. *Swoosh-whoosh*. He looked to Jeremy expectantly.

He tried one tentative swipe. The blade didn't stay level, and he was so afraid of hitting himself on the follow-through. He dropped it halfway through the swing and leaped away. It hit the ground with a *clunk*, bits of snow flying, and lay flat.

"I'm sorry. I got it wet."

"No harm done. Once again."

All the frustrations of the day welled up in Jeremy. "Can't I just go home? You can see I'm bad."

"You would give up after one try? Your kind is being kept from knowing who they really are."

It wasn't a good argument for Asiel to use at the moment. "All they do is laugh at me."

"Are you no better than Jonah?"

"Who? Wait … the guy who got swallowed by a whale?"

"The man who fled in the opposite direction when God directed him to go to the city of Nineva. A storm sank his ship, and the Lord God sent the whale to save and deliver him to where he should have gone. Will you also run from God's command?"

Jeremy's temper flared. "Hey, I didn't ask for this angel thing! It's made my life the pits. As if it wasn't, already. And now God wants me to be a soldier? Hee-yeah. I'm picked last for everything. Doesn't he know that?"

He reached the full-tirade point. "Why am I always picked on? Every school I ever go to, I'm the big joke. Like I really enjoy being the only one who can see demons. And why won't he let Dad come home? Huh? And why should I be the hero? Heroes don't run in the family!"

He was red-faced and wet-eyed. Asiel waited for a long moment, then answered quietly. "Does not the love of Christ move you to serve him?"

"I just want to go home!"

Asiel said no more. The weaponry faded away, leaving the outline of the sword in the snow. The upright oval swimming with the colors and sounds of earth appeared before Jeremy. He stepped into it and found himself back in his own room in Anoka, dressed, once more, in jeans and a sweatshirt.

Mom and Dana were home, but he didn't want them to know he was there. He lay on his bed, staring at crack patterns in the ceiling. He found the one that looked like a bearded lady, and the one that looked like a rabbit.

He heard footsteps drawing near. His door opened. He rolled off the bed and disappeared. Mom pushed in with a laundry basket and froze at the sight of his messed-up bedspread and his body depression in the middle of it.

"Jeremy? Are you here?"

He held his breath.

"Silly," she muttered, plopping the basket on his bed and folding socks.

Dana hurried down the hall. "Who are you talking to, Mom?" she called out.

"Oh, nobody. I thought Jeremy was back."

Dana came in at a trot. "Is he?" She sounded excited, as though she expected to see some great person, not her loser brother. Jeremy's face burned. She scanned the room, bright-eyed, frowning to see it empty. "Maybe he's invisible."

She twirled, her arms wide, making her way from the door to the head of his bed. He leaped in the air, her fingers barely missing his foot.

"Now we're both being silly," said Mom. "How would he get here?"

"He can fly."

"It's seven hundred miles."

"Maybe he quit 'cause of the big scary lady."

"He isn't a quitter."

That made Jeremy's head throb. Mom shoved his old, threadbare socks in his sock drawer and left. Dana tagged along at her heels, sighing, her eyes dulled down.

He sat on the bed and reappeared because it was easier to rest his head on his hands when he could see them. After a long, heavy moment, he raised his eyes and spoke softly. "Can … I go back to Glacier?"

It was a prayer. An oval appeared, swirling with colors and the world's music.

He stepped back out of the travel-way to the mountain meadow. The shadows had grown long. The sun sank behind the mountains. He willed himself to be dressed like an angel again, because he was cold, not because he felt worthy of it.

He knelt in the snow, and his heart broke. "Do you really love me, Lord Jesus?" he cried out. "Do you?"

A soft golden light enveloped him. Had the day still been bright, he wouldn't have seen it. But the deep shadows let him take in the glow, blanketing him on the outside, working its warmth into his core.

Questions leaped up inside him like startled birds caught in a spotlight: Why had Dad made drugs more important than Mom, Dana, and his son? Why, if he said he loved them, did he set them up for ridicule and poverty, crying and worrying? Why couldn't he have been a man like Grandpa—steady and kind? Not that Dad wasn't a nice guy. At his best, he was kindhearted, fun, and funny. So, why did he let his addiction drive him to crime?

Why wasn't he here now, when Jeremy needed him?

He began to cry freely, without worrying about anyone mocking him or fussing over him. His tears flowed, and the questions flew away, one by one. They didn't need answering today.

Today, Jeremy heard the only answer he needed. It took care of everything.

"I love you, my son."

My son! The Lord Jesus Christ, King of Kings, called him his son!

He felt the gentle touch of a hand. He opened his bleary eyes. The golden light seemed brighter. Asiel stood by him, resting his hand on his head.

Jeremy wiped his face and stood as Asiel gently removed his hand. The loyalty wrought by his newfound love flared like a beacon torch. Jeremy went incandescent because of it, along with Asiel, the golden light strong upon him also.

"What was that place called where Jonah was supposed to go?" he asked Asiel.

"Nineva."

"Let's go."

Asiel grinned. A multicolored oval appeared before the two of them.

Chapter 10

KNOW YOUR GENETICS

J EREMY, IN JEANS and dimmed back to normal, stepped from the oval into the third floor room where Prouse believed she held him captive. Asiel, following closely, moved in front of the camera. "This will keep the human enemy from knowing you left."

He aimed his sword and hit it with a narrow beam of lightning. "The less they know, the less they can use. You, on the other hand, must learn all you can."

"Right," mouthed Jeremy. The camera, an hour of its video erased, ran on again.

Jeremy lay on the bed reading a book when Prouse unlocked the door. She took a cautious look in, saw him docile, and made way for Henry who bore a case of bottled water.

"Watcha readin'?" he asked, peering at the book cover. "Hardy Boys. My favorite when I was your age."

"It was either that or *How to Build a Birdhouse,*" said Jeremy flatly.

"Don't you got one of them iPods? So nobody can talk to you?"

"Mine broke."

"I'll have more books brought in," said Prouse. "You must excuse the necessary inconvenience. You have been kept comfortable."

Jeremy kept reading.

"Mona will bring your dinner at six," Henry told him. "You like burritos?"

"Whatever."

Prouse headed back out. "Bring his homework, too."

Henry followed her. The door closed, but the lock didn't click. It opened again. Henry held it for someone pushing a metal cart on wheels full of little gadgets with probes on them and worse, syringes. Jeremy sat up and snapped the book shut.

A pudgy, red-haired nurse wearing a smock with smiley faces on it came with the cart. Prouse stuck her head back in. "Ms. Lund will give you your physical."

She pulled away. The door shut, and the lock clicked. Ms. Lund, with a nurse-like smile, brought her laptop to the table.

"Okay, Jeremy," she said, settling herself in a chair. "Does anyone in your family bleed without stopping?"

He had no idea. He didn't know the answers to most of her questions, yet she typed constantly, her fingers flying. He grew more nervous by the second. He'd had his seventh grade shots. What more could they want? He hated shots!

She took a narrow, stretchy band from a drawer in the cart and tied it around Jeremy's forearm above the elbow. She wiped the fat vein on the underside of his elbow with alcohol. He hated that sharp smell. It usually meant pain was next.

She picked up a fat plastic tube and uncapped it. The sight of the needle gave Jeremy an imaginary sting on his arm. This couldn't be an injection. The tube was empty.

Asiel appeared, startling him so much that he flinched.

"Nothing to be nervous about," said Ms. Lund in the bright, obnoxious voice that nurses can use. "This won't hurt too much."

"Give her none of your blood," Asiel ordered him.

"*How?*" he mouthed.

She brought the needle to his vein.

"My grandma bled a lot," he popped out, off the top of his head. That was probably true. She had been a war prisoner and must have taken lots of beatings.

Lund paused. "She was a hemophiliac?"

She recapped the needle and set the empty blood phial on the cart. The lock rattled and Prouse marched in the room. "Nurse, continue what you were doing."

"But if there's a chance that he …"

"His mother gave no indication of a problem. We must have his blood."

Scowling, Lund picked up the tube and popped off the cap.

"Let it pass through," said Asiel.

"Let it what?" Jeremy began, confused, and then caught himself. He shouldn't be talking to anyone right now.

"It's like a wall coming at you," Asiel added.

Jeremy understood, barely in time. Lund brought the needle to his vein. The point entered without the push and puncture she expected. She blinked, puzzled. She pulled the plunger, but the tube stayed empty.

Her voice grew high-pitched. "What?"

"Defective needle?" asked Prouse, clearly displeased.

Lund snatched another blood tube. The same thing happened. She peered at Jeremy's bulging vein, unmarked by a hole of any kind. It throbbed, and his hand felt cold.

"My hand's going numb," he said.

Lund ripped off the band. His hand tingled, and he rubbed it, busily ignoring Prouse glaring at him like a judge about to hang an outlaw. "What did you do?"

"I'm just sitting here."

"Good answer," said Asiel.

He looked back at her, all innocence. Meanwhile, Lund made short work of gathering her laptop. The women left, one upset and the other smoldering. The lock clicked extra loudly it seemed to Jeremy.

"What's the big deal with my blood?"

"You must find that out," said Asiel, zapping the camera again.

Two hours later, his supper finished and the dishes removed, Jeremy sat at the table poring over the human studies textbook, *Understanding Genetics.* Asiel appeared, reading over his shoulder.

"It says here," said Jeremy, "'some traits, such as red hair, tend to skip generations.' Yeah, but, ten thousand generations?"

"Perhaps your friends will help you find the answers. In which case, you'll be gone for a longer time." Asiel stood, pondering and made a decision. "Barzel?" he called out.

A travel-way appeared overhead, horizontal, running along the ceiling. It had gold, silver, and pure whites rippling across it along with colored sparks of diamonds and other jewels flashing. Jeremy caught a scent of sweet fruit carrying such a delicious smell that anything else on earth smelled like dry cardboard by comparison. Twinkling notes from a harp pierced his heart, and he heard angel voices singing a glorious melody and harmonies woven together.

The angels in heaven were worshipping God, and Jeremy's heart sang with them. He had to join them! He ached to see the temple where the Most High dwelled. He lifted off the floor, rising toward the oval, reaching for it.

Asiel's hands clamped on his shoulders and brought his feet back to the floor. For one dreadful moment, Jeremy felt a rage beyond words.

"I know, little brother," said Asiel gently. "You long for it."

What's more, Jeremy saw an echo of his own yearning for heaven in Asiel's eyes. His anger cooled, but not his longing.

"Wait the allotted time," Asiel urged him.

A lump rose in Jeremy's throat, and his eyes filmed with tears he couldn't explain. Yet, a part of his mind was detached enough to marvel at himself. Why did he feel so homesick for a place he'd never seen?

A blond, curly-haired angel who looked a great deal like Jeremy floated down through the horizontal oval. He had the body and face of a teen and the wisdom of Moses in his eyes.

The heavenly travel-way disappeared and the longing eased a little. Barzel changed his robe to the same jeans and football sweatshirt Jeremy wore. How cool was this?

"The Vikings' fan from heaven!" he joked, partly to lighten himself up.

Barzel looked utterly confused. "The what?"

"Can I use you for other things, too?"

Asiel merely smiled. A familiar, color-washed, earthly doorway appeared up and down to the floor. He nodded at Jeremy to lead. He stepped to the oval and disappeared, Jeremy following.

Barzel moved to the bed and sat on the edge, promptly making a face and standing. The jeans had ridden up. He tugged them back to normal and sat again. "Not very comfortable, human clothing," he muttered.

Epi and Josh were studying at their desks as Jeremy stepped out of the oval, straight into Epi's line-of-sight. He yelled out, startled. They jumped to their feet.

"You can appear out of thin air now?" demanded Epi.

"You didn't see the travel-way?"

"The what?"

"Never mind."

"Prouse told us you were in the sick ward 'cause you had a bad reaction to medicine," said Josh.

Jeremy snorted in disdain. "Liar. Did she take blood samples from you?"

They nodded.

"Haven't you wondered how we got this way?"

"All the time, man," said Epi.

"Then help me figure it out. How did the genes of the Nephilim get into us?"

Josh had also been studying *Understanding Genetics*. Jeremy sat at his desk and flipped to chapter four.

Epi moved to his desk for the same book. "I read about them in Genesis. Took me a while to find those Nephilim guys, 'cause I couldn't remember the chapter number. And there were only, like, two sentences."

Josh sat on his bed. "Where is there a Bible around here?"

"Mona's got one. I asked."

Jeremy planted his finger with a *thump* on a paragraph. "Okay. It says, 'Start with your grandparents.' My mom's mom is really nice. I'd believe it if she had some angel in her, but she couldn't fly, no matter what."

"Too fat?" guessed Epi.

"Yeah."

All three chuckled at that. "So's mine," said Epi.

Josh nodded hard, his grandma was most certainly in the same condition.

Jeremy continued to think while he talked. "My dad's mom, Grandma Josephine, died when I was five.

She was no angel. She could be mean. She slapped my ears once 'cause I spilled a glass of milk, and Dad said she drank like a fish. She did some cool stuff in World War II though. She was a French resistance fighter. She wound up in a German prison camp."

Josh gave a little cry of surprise. "So did my grandpa. His plane was shot down."

"Yeah, mine, too," added Epi, eagerly. "He was a ball turret gunner in a B-17. He sat in this plastic ball thing under the airplane. He said it was so little he could hardly sit up in it. His plane blew up and he got caught in a tree by his parachute. German farmers got 'im and took 'im to a prison camp."

Their one thing in common sank in through a charged silence. "Ask the others," said Jeremy.

Epi ran out the door before he finished the sentence.

Epi dashed back in five minutes later. "It's nine for nine on the guys' floor," he announced.

"Let's ask the girls," said Josh. "Wait. The Man-Lady keeps the halls locked."

Jeremy was smug. "Guys, it's time for you to learn two things the Higher Humanity Institute doesn't know you can do and wouldn't like if it did."

He grabbed Josh's shirt by the back and turned him toward the wall. "Pass through it because you want to."

Josh put on the brakes. "What if I don't? I'm not leaving my face print on the wall!"

"Arm, then."

Jeremy thrust his hand and arm through to the elbow. They mimicked him, grimacing, goggling at the sight of their arms pushed through the plaster, looking cut off.

Jeremy stepped back and shoved Josh through. Epi hopped through of his own accord. In the next second, all three stood in the hall, Epi and Josh laughing in stunned amazement and Jeremy laughing at them. The floor captain's door, three down from theirs, opened. Carl thrust his head out.

"Go invisible," whispered Jeremy. "Just by wanting to."

They vanished. Carl looked their way, saw nothing, and gave up, closing his door.

Josh laughed, keeping it soft. "How cool is this?"

"Will yourself not to be heard," said Jeremy. "We don't want the others to know we can do this. It's not time, yet."

"Girl's floor," said Josh.

Footsteps moved toward the stairs. There was the *thunk* of someone stumbling and a grunt from Epi. "I just tripped myself. Can't see my feet, how'm I s'posed to walk?"

"Get used to it," said Josh, sounding as if he'd been walking invisibly for years.

Jeremy heard someone reach the stairs. Brisk footsteps started down. Suddenly there was a *yelp* and a series of thumps.

"Did you fall and die?" cried out Epi.

"I caught the rail," said Josh, panting. "I think I'll slow down now."

Jeremy took to the air with a gentle swish, passed them both, and came down on the landing below. "Guys," he reminded them. "We can fly."

There were dual moans above him as they grieved their stupidity. He heard two more swishes. Then Epi's voice rang out in fright. "Yeah, but how do you land when you can't see your feet?"

Jeremy had the sense to get off the landing, floating down five steps. He waited. He heard a smack and a thud.

"Ow, man!" griped Epi.

Josh moaned. "That was my head!"

"Get used to it," said Jeremy.

Tameeka helped them round up all the HHI girls. Like it or not, they were crammed into the girls' TV lounge, scrunched on the couch and easy chairs or sitting on the floor. Rachel stood by the door. Jeremy leaned against a wall, invisible. After all, he was supposed to be locked up in Walker Hall.

Josh sat on the floor in the middle of the room using a borrowed pen and paper for taking notes. He explained that the seventh grade boys were doing research for human studies, which was true as far as it went.

"Mrs. Prouse doesn't give extra credit," said Melissa, suspiciously.

Epi turned scornful for one second sounding just like Sharp. "We're doing it for the joy of learning."

Josh questioned them one by one and their answers made Jeremy's heart thump. Every HHI student so far had one grandparent who had been a Nazi prisoner. He saved the worst then the best for last. "Okay, Melissa."

She had a tight frown on her face, hating this. "Yeah, my grandma was in a death camp. The Nazis killed her sisters. We're Jewish." She clamped her mouth closed against saying anything else.

"Then why don't you believe in angels?" asked Epi.

"Where was God when they took my aunts to the gas chambers?"

Epi shrugged. "It wasn't God who built those things."

"That's the connection, then," said Josh, speaking fast. "Rachel, how 'bout you?"

But she was no longer in the room.

"Maybe she had to go," said Epi helpfully.

"Want me to go to the bathroom and ask her?" offered Tameeka.

"Sure," said Josh.

She flitted out of the room.

Three street lamps weren't enough to illuminate the campus, which was just how Scrag liked it. He chuckled, watching Rachel fly through the shadows toward her grandmother's lighted office on the second floor of Walker Hall. He could see the woman through the window, working at her desk. Rachel flew fast, her arms stretched to the full and her hands in tight fists. Of course, she was frightened, with his eyes on her!

He flew after her at an easy pace. She landed outside the front door. The witless girl didn't know that she could pass through walls. He touched down behind her as she reached for the brass bar handle. She shivered.

It was his breath on her neck that chilled her. She pushed down the bar and hurried inside before the door even opened a quarter of the way. He followed her, taking his time.

Jeremy stepped back into the Walker Hall third floor room. He could've made an easy escape right then. It made him want to laugh, but he also wondered how long the charade would need to continue.

Barzel waited patiently on the edge of the bed. He rose and joined Jeremy out of the camera's view. "An older man brought your suitcase," he said. "That's what he called it."

"They're keeping me in here."

An oval appeared in the ceiling. Barzel rose and disappeared through it. Longing welled in Jeremy once more, and he lifted off toward it, but the oval disappeared before he was two inches off the floor. It was devastating. If Mom had slammed and locked the apartment door in his face, it couldn't have felt any worse.

He may as well get ready for bed. He washed his face, brushed his teeth, and had just pulled on his pajamas when the door clicked and opened. Henry entered with two stacked cots, set them down, and left with only a smile for an explanation.

He came right back in with two suitcases and Epi and Josh following behind. A maintenance man named Chuck, his body as beefy as his name suggested, came in with bedding and pillows bulging in his arms. He dropped them in heaps on the cots. The men left. Henry was still smiling as he locked them in.

"I think we're in jail," said Epi.

Chapter 11

SPIES

JEREMY FLAPPED WITH all his strength, desperate to escape the pterodactyl racing after him. He reached the end of his apartment hallway, banking hard over the stairwell.

Plunk! Something hit him in the chest. It was a human studies textbook, thrown by the Man-Lady ...

Someone shook him by the shoulder. He surged awake to find a folded newspaper on his chest and Asiel standing at his bedside. Jeremy raised his head, too groggy to get out a word. Epi and Josh snored into their pillows.

Asiel pulled open one side of the curtains, letting in fire-colored light from the rising sun. Epi blinked awake at a sun shaft in his face. He raised his head toward the window, frowning, to see the other half of the curtains slide open by itself. He let out a yell.

Josh awoke in time to watch the newspaper rise from Jeremy's chest and unfold, seemingly by itself.

Jeremy had to laugh at the looks on their faces. "It's the school ghost."

"This is no time for joking." Asiel held the headline at Jeremy's eye level. "Read."

He obeyed. The headline made him sit up and swing his feet to the floor. He turned the front page toward his roommates and snapped the paper open. They saw huge, bold words: "FLYING TEENS THE FIRST HIGHER HUMANS?"

Rachel hovered under the headline, her picture covering half the page. It was the same photo Prouse had sent to Jeremy in her HHI invitation letter.

Asiel zapped the camera. If the other two had any doubts about Jeremy's angel, the thin line of lightning arcing from mid-air to the camera convinced them.

"The war for truth is starting," said Asiel.

Mona brought hot cereal, scrambled eggs, toast, juice, and oranges for their breakfast. Prouse came in after she left and towered over the boys as they busied themselves with spreading PB and J on their toast.

She grilled them like an army officer. "Why were you asking the others if they had war-prisoner grandparents?"

"Homework," said Josh. He'd taken a mouthful of oatmeal so the word came out muffled.

"Don't lie."

"It was, though," said Epi.

Jeremy took such a huge bite out of his toast that he could only nod his head.

She studied them, narrow-eyed. "I did not assign group research. You were to ponder your ancestry on your own."

"But, we thought it'd help us learn." Josh managed to sound hurt.

She didn't buy it. "Do you still believe you're Nephilim?"

No one answered her. She could just as well have asked them, "Do you still believe you're human?"

She planted her hands on the table, bringing her face close. "If you're going to keep insisting on this half-angel nonsense, you'll remain here. Mr. Bock will tutor you."

Anger rose in Jeremy, his innocent façade cracking fast. "I want to call my Mom."

"I called her. I told her you're disruptive." And on that note of triumph, Prouse marched out, closing the lock with a strong clack for an exclamation point.

"Let's just leave," said Epi.

Jeremy glared at him to shut-up, flicking his eyes toward the camera. "We gotta find some answers," he said, low-voiced. "Why is the Man-Lady so ticked off that we found out about our grandparent connection? It must be important."

Tameeka appeared beside the table, dressed in the HHI phys-ed outfit.

Josh, badly startled, bumped his orange juice glass. He made a grab and spilled half of it, splotching an orange wet patch onto the tablecloth. "Whoa! You like causing heart attacks? How did you get in here?"

"I believe we part angel. So, I asked myself, what are all the things an angel can do? And then I did 'em. I passed through my wall, and I went invisible. I followed the Man-Lady. And yeah, our grandparent connection is really important."

"How did she find out we asked everybody about it?" asked Jeremy. "Do you know?"

Tameeka's air of self-satisfaction faded a bit. "Yeah."

"Melissa ratted on us. Right?"

"No."

Jeremy waited. Tameeka took a deep breath and spilled it. "Rachel told her."

That hurt like a punch from Sid Lundahl.

"How do you know she meant anything bad by it?" began Josh, reasoning. "Maybe the Man-Lady told Rachel to tell her if any of us asked around about our grandparents, without saying why she wanted to know."

That eased the sting a little.

"I mean, if I had the Man-Lady for my grandma …"

"Ee-yuck!" put in Epi.

"So, let's go," said Tameeka, as bossy as ever.

Josh turned peevish. "Go where?" he snarled.

"Prouse's office. We need answers. It's the best place to start at."

"In the first place, who says we want to be spies? In the second place, who made you the commanding officer?"

Tameeka bristled. "I get a good idea an' it makes me a general, all of a sudden?"

Before Josh could fire back an answer, Jeremy, who agreed with her, made his sword-and-scabbard materialize at his hip. It derailed Josh and Tameeka's disagreement nicely. They stared, open-mouthed.

Epi was about to kill off his orange juice, but he set the glass down in a hurry. Jeremy moved to the camera, pulled the sword free, and zapped it. He replaced it and turned to the others.

Tameeka closed her eyes and concentrated. Nothing happened. She stared at her still-empty hip, frowning in confusion.

"I don't think you can give yourselves weapons, yet," said Jeremy in a whisper. The camera was running again. "I'm kinda like … enlisted. You can help me spy, though."

He took aim at the camera and hit it with a beam from his sword, just to make sure that Prouse couldn't guess what they were up to.

They passed through the floor to save time, since Jeremy wasn't sure if the others could use an earthly travel-way. The Science Lab happened to be underneath their jail room, empty of students at this hour. Mr. Bock sat at his desk grading upper-level test papers and giving his watch anxious glances.

Epi wanted to see what score his brother got, but Jeremy kept him moving. They spoke in sign language, five feet above the floor. He'd told them to make themselves visible to each other but invisible to everyone else.

Flying by the desk, they created a breeze that ruffled Bock's papers. He frowned toward the closed window. Josh couldn't resist hovering over a cage and scratching his favorite rat's back. The startled animal nearly bit him for it, whipping its head around and snapping at the finger it couldn't see. Josh jerked his hand away, rattling it against the cage. Bock looked up again.

Stop playing around, Jeremy mouthed at him.

They moved into the hall. A brass nameplate on the door clearly marked Prouse's office, as if Jeremy didn't know that door by heart. They passed in.

He half expected to see Scrag looming over the file. Thankfully, they were alone.

"Somebody should watch the hall," whispered Epi. "You want me to?"

Jeremy spoke loudly, just to rattle him. "We don't need to whisper. Just don't want to be heard, and you can sing the 'Star Spangled Banner,' if you feel like it."

"Then why didn't you talk out loud to me around Mr. Bock?" asked Josh.

"Because you might not have chosen not to be heard."

Josh had to think about that. Meanwhile, Jeremy scanned the room. "Let's see. There's her desk, the closet, and the file cabinet."

"I'll start with the desk," said Tameeka. "What we lookin' for?"

"I guess anything about German war prisoners," answered Jeremy. "Papers, pictures, experiments …"

"Experiments?" echoed Epi. "That's gruesome."

"Yeah," said Jeremy soberly. "Nazi scientists did medical experiments on their prisoners. Grandma was one of them. She told Dad some things when she was drunk. They gave her lots of shots." He shuddered. "She hated going to doctors ever since."

He moved to the closet, found it locked, and passed through the door, Josh at his heels. Tameeka stuck her face through the top of Prouse's desk and searched the main drawer.

"Okay, I'm lookout," announced Epi. He thrust his upper body through the hallway wall, looking like the boy who was eaten by a wall.

Henry strolled past. Epi couldn't resist blowing at his bald spot. He touched his head and looked up, trying to spot the cobweb or whatever had brushed him. Epi waved his arms at him.

With a frown, Henry went on his way.

In the Walker Hall lobby, the floors and banisters gleamed. Mrs. Prouse held up a copy of the same newspaper Asiel had shown the boys, displaying her granddaughter's picture and the headline. Her students applauded, the noise bouncing off the marble and granite. Rachel beamed and blushed.

"Youngsters," Prouse declared. "Today is the most important day of your lives. The world media is arriving to film you making history!"

The teens clapped again. Sharp, unimpressed, frowned toward the seventh graders. Four of them were missing, his younger brother among the absentees.

Jeremy's and Josh's heads and hands were stuck in the top drawer of the black file cabinet. Jeremy made the index finger on his left hand glow, for a light.

"I need to learn that," said Josh.

Jeremy rifled through the files. He stopped at a fat one, muttering. "The title's in German, and it's got the number twelve on it."

He gripped it with both hands and started to lift it out. It hit the bottom of the upper drawer. His hands passed through. The file stopped with a *clunk* and dropped back into place.

"Dumb! I forgot. We can't make something pass through something else just 'cause we're holding it."

"Spread it on top of the other files, then."

Jeremy did so. Tameeka stuck her face in, crowding the drawer, irritating Josh. They read eagerly by the odd, white light of Jeremy's finger. He saw a name and pointed to it with his unlit right index finger. "Gustave Praus! Must be a relative of hers."

"It ain't spelled the same," argued Tameeka.

"She must've Americanized it."

"Look at all the chemical formulas," said Josh.

Jeremy was getting excited. "Here! This word. *Nevilim*. Here and here. Isn't 'v' pronounced 'f' in German?"

"I dunno," said Josh.

"Yeah," cut in Tameeka. "My Aunt Coreena got herself a bug, an' she told me that in Germany it's pronounced *'Folksvagen.'*"

"That word is 'Nephilim,' then."

"What does this mean?" asked Josh.

Tameeka flipped the pages back to the front of the report. "See the swastika? This Praus guy was like a Nazi scientist, or a doctor, or somethin' ..."

"That's why the Man-Lady looks like a German prison guard," said Josh, sounding triumphant. He deepened his voice. "Boyz unt girlz, you vill not belief in angelz!"

"Heil!" barked Tameeka and snapped her arm up, mocking the Nazi salute.

They'd paid attention to their grandparents' stories enough to make fun of America's old enemy.

Jeremy mulled aloud. "Okay, so the Nazis were the ones Asiel told me about. They found the Nephilim corpses. They … made a formula, put it in our grandparents … and we inherited it."

"A formula from corpses? That's too gross!" said Tameeka. "An' they put that in my grandpa? Eesh!"

Jeremy felt warmth grow inside him, and he knew the source. He was on the right track. He also had a strong sense of what to do—a command without words. "We gotta get this report out of here."

"Why?" asked Josh.

"Because it proves that we really are Nephilim," said Tameeka, quick on the uptake.

"Okay, but how? You just said we can't make it pass through the locked drawer."

They needed a plan. Jeremy locked his eyes on the report, thinking hard …

Epi's voice broke in sharply. "The Man-Lady's coming!"

They pulled away from the file. Prouse unlocked the office door and came in. She was actually smiling. She set the newspaper on her desk, her granddaughter's front-page photo grinning up at her. "My pretty star."

Jeremy agreed with her and would've stared at the picture. But something Prouse wore caught his eye. He pointed at it.

Prouse wore a file key on a stout chain around her neck.

After she left, Jeremy stated, "We're getting that key off her."

Epi gave a quiet whistle. "Like we can just take it off her neck?"

"Doesn't she have class right now?"

That raised a squawk from Tameeka. "No classes today! The reporters are here. I'm supposed to be at the field."

"Get going," Jeremy ordered her.

She flew through the outside wall. The boys hesitated for half a breath before they took off after her.

The media arrived in droves, many in news vans. Epi, Josh, and Jeremy flew unseen over school lots filled with vehicles marked "CNN," "FOX NEWS," "ABC," "NBC," "CBS." They were all here.

There were VIP guests in luxury cars and limousines and parents in minivans. They took up every parking place on campus and parked in lines along the driveway. Prouse had Henry shuttle them in the HHI van. She'd thought of everything by the looks of things.

Jeremy spotted CHANNEL 5 NEWS from Minneapolis and saw the silver head of Lee Englestad walking to the reporters' place along the Athletics Field. That made sense; an Anoka and a Plymouth boy were making worldwide news. Mr. Englestad would be disappointed then, Jeremy realized with a pang of regret, so would Mom and Dana. No Minnesota boy would appear on camera today.

Jeremy made for an oak tree at the edge of the field, opposite the audience, and landed on a fat branch. Epi chose the next branch up and Josh settled on the tree's wide "Y". Gloom draped over all three of them. "I'd like to fly on TV," said Epi.

That made the sting worse for Jeremy. "I'm the reason you're missing it."

"I wonder if Rachel's going to go bright for them," said Josh.

The HHI students stood in lines by classes just inside the woods, out of direct sight of the reporters. Jeremy saw Tameeka materialize behind them. She sneaked her way into the seventh grader line. She released a sigh of relief that Jeremy could see from where he sat.

Rachel gave her a hug. Lucky Tameeka.

Scrag had gloating to do. He passed into the Walker Hall third floor room, intent on harassing Jeremy. He toyed with appearing to the other two, for the fun of frightening human children half out of their wits.

The three boys sat on each of their beds. Wait … something wasn't right. For one thing, they all saw him and showed no fright. For another, he felt their power and the Presence of Holiness that reviled him horribly. These were no mere boys!

Snarling, he drew his sword. In the next split second, white gowns and weaponry replaced the human garb. The three leaped to their feet and drew their swords as one: *s-s-shing*.

He roared and fled through the hallway wall. He was a vicious fighter, but three against one—and the one surprised—made the odds a bit uncomfortable. Regroup!

He had a task to do. In a rage, he flew with great speed to the woman. She needed to know her prisoners had escaped, and if they'd bothered to use angel look-a-likes, they planned to go back to their jail room as though they'd never left. But what were they up to in the meantime?

On the Athletics Field, ringed by spectators and the media, all cameras and microphones pointed at Louisa Prouse who looked commanding in a burgundy suit. Her hair looked stiffer than usual, and her makeup was so thick that Jeremy could see her features from halfway down the field.

She was in her glory. "This is nothing less than a changing point in history, ladies and gentlemen," she thundered into a tinny-sounding microphone plugged into the school's portable amp. "And here they are! My wonderful students! The first to reach humanity's next level!"

With that, the HHI students ran onto the field, their dark-blue gym outfits freshly laundered and spiffy. Triumphant music, rocky and young sounding, pounded from outdoor speakers. They took off in a "V" formation, Rachel leading them, and flew around the field at a hundred feet up. The audience applauded and shouted. Moms wiped tears.

The women in the crowd broke into astonished shrieks as Rachel and a handful of other teens went incandescent. The fliers broke into smaller formations to zoom and dart through the slalom course and whap the targets, making them whirl. Carl and another tenth grader swooshed basketballs through the hoops from twenty feet above them.

Most of the teens loved it. Tameeka, however, looked belligerent, as though she was obeying, yeah, but she didn't have to like it. Carl looked bothered about something. A key flyer was missing from the older boys' formation. He threw a question at a classmate in passing, and Jeremy caught the words: "Where's Sharp?"

The other tenth grader shrugged.

"Yeah, where's he gone to?" Epi muttered, staring all around him as though he hoped to catch sight of Sharp somewhere on campus.

To make matters worse, Scrag appeared beside Prouse and slapped her shoulder. She flinched, but remained caught up in the show of her own making.

What was he doing here? This couldn't be good. He growled something at her. She sent a frown toward Walker Hall.

"Go!" Scrag bellowed. "The captives!"

What about the captives? Jeremy tensed, seeing that Scrag's words spurred the Man-Lady into action, though she probably didn't hear a thing. Her inner urgency showed on her face. Definitely not good!

Mr. Bock tapped his foot, thoroughly enjoying the spectacle. Prouse said something to him. He nodded, too engrossed to give her a glance.

She hurried away, Scrag at her heels, until he broke away and flew toward her office. She strode for the Walker Hall main entrance.

Jeremy knew what was called of him. Keep an eye on the enemy. Yeah, but which of his enemies should he follow?

Prouse stepped into the third-floor room. The three boys sat on their beds. She felt a pulse of anger for giving into paranoia and missing out on her triumph. She looked closer.

They didn't give her a glance. She moved toward them, and they ducked their faces. Her anger surged now. She grabbed Jeremy's chin and lifted it. The boy looking back at her had Jeremy's blond curls, but the eyes were as piercing as sunlight on water and not a teen's eyes, either. They held a daunting wisdom and power that, for one moment, made her catch her breath and want to back away.

She held her ground, dropping the chin and taking in the other two, who were certainly not Epifano Ruiz and Joshua Bergren, as closely as they resembled them.

"Who are you?" she barked at Jeremy's stand-in. "Where are they?"

None answered. She exited fast, making certain to lock the door.

Henry sat in a folding chair near the jail room door, reading a newspaper. He stood hastily to the stiletto clicking of his boss's shoes, the pace telling him she was upset.

She was ashen with anger. "Phase Two," she snapped, and sailed by him like a battleship, taking the stairs at a breakneck pace for a woman whose narrow heels bore as much weight as hers did.

As entertaining a spectacle as it made, he knew better than to waste time. He pulled a walkie-talkie off his belt, pushing the button as he walked. "Henry to Chuck. We're going."

"Okay," answered Chuck through the hissing static.

Henry headed down the stairs at a fast clip.

Scrag passed into the Man-Lady's office through the outer wall. He seemed utterly unaware that three Nephilim boys tailed him. They'd willed themselves to be invisible to all eyes but their own. Jeremy prayed it would work. Could a demon see another spirit being all the time? He'd find out.

He hesitated at the office wall, scared to face the monster. "You think the Man-Lady went to our jail?" Epi asked him. "Why didn't we follow her?"

"We're following one of her … workers. He's in there right now," said Jeremy, his heart squeezing.

"Henry? Sweet, man! Let's spy on him."

Before Jeremy could stop him, Epi flew through the office wall. Jeremy hesitated, knowing he should go after him. It was the last thing he wanted to do.

He had no time to decide. Epi shrieked, the sound muffled by the wall, and burst outside at comet speed, Scrag hot on his heels.

Josh saw the demon, too. He yelled and flew away as though a host of demons chased him.

If Jeremy didn't do something, Scrag would have Epi in his claws. He raced after them, leading with his sword.

Scrag wheeled around advancing at Jeremy, drawing his black sword. "I'll cut your arms off."

He struck. Jeremy swatted back. His hands felt like lead blocks. *Clank*! Their blades hit. The shock jarred Jeremy to his shoulders. His sword spun from his hands in flashes of silver and gold.

Jeremy turned to race away. Scrag made a point-on thrust, aiming to run him through the ribs. Asiel appeared. His blade turned the stroke. Scrag surged back from him, his shield raised.

"You won't get that report," he vowed, gloating. "I'll guard it with a hundred of my best soldiers. And who will be warrior enough to get it?"

He sneered at Jeremy. "Your guard dog here isn't allowed to steal human items. That means you'll have to fight me for it. You, half-breed!"

He roared with laughter. "You're pathetic!"

The light came on in Prouse's office. Scrag back-flapped toward it. "I'd love to keep playing, but her business is my business. She wishes it." He disappeared into her office.

Asiel lowered his sword with a sigh. "And she doesn't even believe that demons exist."

Jeremy watched through the window as Prouse rushed to the cabinet and unlocked the top drawer. She yanked up Report Number Twelve and rifled through it. It was intact, of course. She sagged with relief. Then she locked the door and left.

Three squat demons appeared in front of the file cabinet. Jeremy moaned at the sight of them, armed to the fangs. And there were millions more where these came from.

"Find your friends," said Asiel. "Then go back to your jail room."

Jeremy turned to leave. Scrag, watching through the window, wasn't finished with his fun for the day. He thrust his head out the office wall.

"You won't get that report, loser!" he yelled at Jeremy's back. And for one nasty second, he spoke with Sid Lundahl's voice. Jeremy grimaced.

Asiel caught him by the shoulders, keeping Scrag from the pleasure of seeing the pain on his face. "Retrieve your sword," he commanded him. "And don't listen to him."

Chapter 12

THREATS

EPI LANDED TO the rear of Walker Hall, hidden by evergreen shrubbery. He leaned against the building, so scared he was almost sick. The bushes rustled. He wheeled to face them, wild-eyed, his hands in fists—as if he could fight that demon thing.

It was Sharp. Epi gasped in relief and flopped back against the wall.

"*Perrillo*, what's she doing to you?" demanded Sharp.

"She's evil, I'm telling you! She's got a demon for a flunky. For real. Thing's got claws and wings, man, and fangs like a vampire. It jumped me."

The fearful memory cut off his voice. He tottered. Sharp surged from the bushes and gripped his shoulders. "Just go home. I saw you come out through the wall. We can do that, man? Why hang around?"

"Gotta help my friends. Gotta fight *el Diablo.*"

"You don't gotta do nothing."

A voice cut into their argument. Jeremy, invisible, had just made his way to the back of Walker Hall. "Epi. Asiel wants us back in our room."

That startled Sharp as badly as he had startled Epi. "Hey, where are you hiding?"

"He's invisible," said Epi.

Sharp's eyes popped wide. "Holy—!"

"Gotta go." Epi disappeared, which did nothing to calm his brother. He lifted off with a gentle swish that Sharp heard.

"Perrillo!" he yelled. "You don't gotta do nothing."

The three boys materialized in the third-floor room. Epi and Josh made beelines for their beds, flopping down to clear their heads of the worst frights they'd ever had.

"What does *perrillo* mean?" Jeremy asked, hoping to distract them.

"Puppy," said Epi. "He always calls me that. I wish he didn't know we can go through walls and go invisible and stuff. He could do things, man."

"What things?"

"He's a homey." Epi let that ominous fact hang in the air.

Josh sat up. "Is it a bad gang?"

Epi grimaced in scorn as though he'd asked the dumbest question on the planet. "They're called the *Cortadors*. The Cutters."

"Bad," said Josh in awe.

A private jet's engines revved up on the first of two short runways at Leesville Airport, so small its terminal only had two gates. The windy roar echoed through the surrounding woods and farm fields.

The blue HHI van pulled up to the terminal. Henry and Chuck hopped out, luggage in their hands and coats draped over their arms. They ran for the jet. The van pulled away.

Since they needed to keep Prouse in the dark about their spying, the three boys stayed put, stuck in the jail room like hamsters in a cage, knowing that someone watched them at all times. Jeremy and Josh competed at a kill-the-monsters video game. Epi fell asleep. It was lunchtime.

The lock clattered and the door opened. They expected to see Mona pushing the cart. Instead,

Jeremy's heart gave a twist. Rachel and Tameeka wheeled it in together.

"Mona's letting us bring your lunch," said Rachel. "Lasagna. And you should see how many people are crammed in the dining room. We students had to eat in the hallway. It's crazy!"

Epi sat up.

"We feel really bad that you guys are sick and had to miss all the fun," she rattled on.

Anger at the lie Prouse told the other students surged in Jeremy, and he wondered why Rachel ratted on him.

Tameeka, unusually quiet, did not attempt to break in. The girls wheeled the cart to the table and made quick work of setting the boys' places while Rachel jabbered. "It's so exciting. All those reporters. I thought I'd mess up. We brought you some candy, too, though Mona thought you may not want it if you're sick."

Jeremy cut her off, surprising even himself with his anger. "We're not sick. We're a threat. We've been locked up because Mrs. Prouse is angry that we found out about the HHI connection to the Nazis. Somebody told her that we asked everybody if their grandparents had been in a German prison camp."

Silence hung between them. Tameeka set the covered food dishes on the table, still saying nothing. When Rachel faced the boys, she looked uncomfortable and—no denying it—guilty. "Sh-she's my grandma. She asked me to tell her right away if anyone ever asked the students the questions you asked. I didn't know what it was about. I never thought she'd lock you up."

She dropped her eyes.

Clack, clack, clack! The unwelcome sound of those hard heels drew near. Prouse's voice carried in from the hallway. "Mona? Why have you left this door open?"

She marched in, freezing at the sight of the three boys she'd imprisoned in the first place back in jail, and the two girls serving them.

"I asked Mona if we could bring them their lunch," explained Rachel in a hurry. With that, she and Tameeka rushed out of the room.

Prouse rounded on Jeremy. "Who were your little friends? Your identical twins? And how did they get in here?"

Jeremy answered coolly. "You won't believe me if I tell you."

She glared him down, and he gave it right back. He watched her push back her rage enough to speak, her voice shaking. "I've waited all my life for this day. The world will finally understand that there are no angels or demons or heaven or hell …"

"We can talk to reporters, too."

"You will stay under lock and key."

"But the world wants to believe in angels at Christmas."

Her face was almost burgundy. "If you leave this room again …"

"You can't keep us here over Christmas break. My mom—"

"Your mother and sister are being watched by my men," Prouse thundered. "If you cross me, your family will die in a burglary-gone-wrong."

That shot Jeremy down from confident to horror struck. He could only stare at her, white-faced and out of words.

Her anger turned to chiding. "Such a tragedy. Both of them shot by unknown assailants. But then, with your father being what he is, it's no surprise that bad types are drawn to your place."

She shifted her attack to Epi and Josh, her volume back to normal, her eyes glinting. "I have men watching your homes as well."

"*Asesinos?*" breathed Epi. "Killers?"

She was enjoying herself royally. "Oh, and that hoodlum brother of yours is missing. He'd better not cause me trouble."

She let the threat hang like black smoke in the air for a moment, then left, slamming the door and locking it.

Epi clutched his head and sat hard on his bed. Josh flopped down, looking sick.

Jeremy did two things: he caused his sword to appear at his side and he made an upright, earthly oval appear. "Missouri to Minnesota in a millisecond. Let's see how her men like this."

Asiel materialized, blocking him.

"Don't stop me," Jeremy snapped at him.

"You're not ready. You must be trained to fight."

"Our families …"

"… are safe as long as you appear to obey the enemy."

Epi and Josh, following Jeremy's stare, were looking straight at Asiel, had they known it. "Are you talking to … to … ?" faltered Epi.

Caught up in the argument, Jeremy ignored him. "What! Let them win?"

"I said appear to obey. Eat now. You need your strength. Then we train."

Asiel was clearly not going to budge from blocking the travel way. Jeremy shut his eyes hard to quell his anger. He opened them, released a breath, and then moved to his seat at the table. "Asiel wants us to eat our lunch," he snapped. He sat hard, his scabbard clunking against the table leg.

The other two joined him without a word, in awe over their unseen guest. They dished up, taking great care not to spill anything.

"Trust and learn," said Asiel. "Hold fast. The lies can't last." Even so, grief crossed his face. "Pray for those whose souls will be darkened."

Chapter 13

WAR

THE NEWS REPORTS stating that the flying teens of the Higher Humanity Institute may be the first human beings to reach a higher stage of development launched the world into a storm. Church leaders all the way up to the Pope demanded to know if the footage was real. Pastors and priests the world over were bombarded with terrified questions from their congregations.

Non-religious people publicly crowed and wrote scathing articles against all religions, countered, of course, by answering write-ups from religion experts. Talk show hosts harangued and political debaters shouted each other down on show after show.

Christians and Jews met in their houses of worship for emergency prayer services and wept before God. Moslems bowed their faces to the earth. Buddhists and Hindus hurried to their temples. Priests and ministers doggedly lit their candles, taught their classes, visited their sick, held their worship services, and continued the routines of Advent.

For some, the rituals, verses, praise songs, and carols had suddenly gone cold. For others, they never meant more to their hearts.

O Come, O Come Emmanuel, and ransom Captive Israel that mourns in lonely exile here until the Son of God appear ...

Then the protests started. Across the United States and Europe, devout believers marched around newspaper headquarters and television stations bearing signs that shouted "GOD IS STILL GOD!" Anti-religious people showed up in droves with signs yelling "GOD IS DEAD!"

Those who hated the church marched around churches with signs of triumph: "NO MORE CHAINS!" And "RELIGION IS A LIE!" Believers arrived, their signs proclaiming "FLYING TEENS ARE A MIRACLE" and "GOD IS REAL!"

The first riot happened at night outside a red brick church in St. Louis. Its tall white steeple, topped by a cross, had been a landmark for a hundred years. For fifty years, the church displayed a hand-painted, ceramic nativity scene on its front lawn lit by spotlights. The wooden stable was hand-built by a carpenter of the congregation. He'd bolted three ceramic angels to the roof. The stable held figurines of cattle, sheep, a donkey and two doves, four shepherds, the three kings, and of course, the holy family with baby Jesus wrapped snuggly in a white ceramic blanket lying on fresh, shiny straw that the same farmer had supplied for thirty years.

Missouri's first snowfall of the season blanketed the lawn and the stable roof, although the church custodian had been careful to brush it off the figures. The anti-religion protesters, two hundred strong, arrived at seven that evening and marched around the parking lot, waving their signs under the light posts and chanting, their breaths showing white. At twenty degrees, icy moisture in the air sank to their bones, making even the warmly dressed people feel like they weren't wearing coats.

The congregation was expecting them, and the cry went out by phone and text messages: Gather at the church with your signs ASAP! Other churches joined the call. By eight, over four hundred Christians circled the church, wearing the snow away to a green path of wilted grass and brown leaves where their course had to leave the sidewalks.

The media arrived, lighting the lot and the lawn as brightly as a sporting event, training their cameras on all the action they could find and hustling to interview anyone willing to talk.

The churchgoers sang rousing praise choruses. Their opponents shouted insults in rhythm. The nativity scene stood in its own, quiet, de-militarized zone unfazed by human noise, until a man lost his temper at the sight of the figures. He rushed at Joseph and kicked him hard in the side. The figure swayed, but did not fall. The original carpenter had put wooden braces on the figures to keep them standing in strong winds.

This wind was a hurricane. Four men from the opposing line rushed him before he could topple the manger. They tackled him to the ground. Anti-religion protesters rushed to his aid. Within moments, the singing turned to screams and the chants to shouts. Fighters on each side rushed to vent their fury with feet and fists.

One camera operator made it a point to station himself near the stable. The rioters pushed it over, at last, and he captured the image of an angel lying shattered on the frozen ground.

It had been six days since the students of the Higher Humanity Institute had flown for the world. The girls sat in their lounge watching the news, since they'd seen each other on TV every day since.

Before this, they'd giggled, teased, and cheered. Tonight, they watched the riot in somber silence. More riots had broken out across the US today, in the aftermath of the battle in front of the St. Louis church. Anger, like a strong infection, swept the country.

The scene returned to that first fight. A frantic mom snatched her little girl out of the way before a writhing pack of fighters trampled her.

And there lay that broken angel. Tameeka burst into tears and could not keep her sobbing quiet.

"What's with you?" Melissa asked her.

Tameeka blasted her answer back. "We caused this!"

She hurried out of the room.

Bright moonlight caused millions of sparkles to glisten across the snow, and where Asiel and Jeremy worked, the glows they gave off turned the sparkles as bright as diamonds.

They'd covered their swords with a gauzy netting sent from heaven that form-fit the blades and allowed no cutting whatever during training. It was as light as tissue and as strong as tank armor. The swords met in ringing *clinks,* their hits so fast the sound was almost continuous.

"Raise your shield higher," Asiel commanded Jeremy. "That's it. Now thrust under."

Jeremy raised his shield a little and shoved his sword forward. Asiel countered with a jab, but Jeremy expected it. He did a strong swipe and twist, knocking Asiel's sword from his hand. It spun and landed blade-down in the snow. *Chunk*!

Asiel roared with laughter. "Much better!"

Jeremy doubled over, panting. "I get so tired, though."

"You're strengthening by the day."

Jeremy sheathed his sword. His shield had a long strap on it that let him hang it across his back or on a shoulder. He draped it over his left shoulder like a purse and leaned against a birch. "We're supposed to leave for Christmas break in two days. So, what's the Man-Lady gonna do?"

"Battle draws near."

"We have a plan to get the file key from her."

"That's good. Just remember: humans can harm humans and angels and demons can harm each other, but neither angels nor demons can kill a human being. Not in this age."

"Then why are people so scared of demons?"

"They can cause minor injuries, such as scratches, giving terror to those who can't see them."

"Hee-yeah!" Jeremy shuddered at the thought of such an attack.

"They can oppress people with bitterness or sadness. They can possess those who let them, in the worst extreme, and use them as their puppets."

"Eeyugh!"

"Such a thing will never happen to those who resist them in any way. You're fine."

"I'm glad to hear it," said Jeremy.

"Mostly, they use the power of the lie. They can drive humans to such despair that they'll kill themselves."

"Doesn't all this mean that Scrag can't hurt me?"

"You're part angel."

Enough said. Jeremy shivered again. Asiel, meanwhile, picked a glowing ring the size of a Frisbee off the snow and hung it on a branch stub.

Jeremy moaned. He knew very well what the ring meant, though Asiel made a point of announcing it. "Target practice."

Asiel walked away, pulling his bow off his shoulder. Jeremy pushed himself from the trunk, sending a dirty look at his back and reaching for his own bow, slung across his back.

At one hundred yards away, Jeremy leaned his shield against a nearby trunk, put an arrow to the string, set his eyes on his mark, and drew, his arms throbbing. He released, the twang a sharp music he loved. His arrow *hizzed* past the target tree, to rattle the underbrush in the woods beyond.

"What do you call that?" Asiel chided him, smiling.

"Needing time to rest."

"Time is running out."

Jeremy's arm was so tired it trembled. They'd practiced swordplay for an hour straight!

"Pray for strength," said Asiel.

He did so, and felt his heart lift. He grabbed and set his arrow to the string in one smooth movement, set his eye on ring-center, drew, and let fly. His arrow whacked inside the ring, slightly to the left of center.

"Beautiful!" gloated Asiel. "You've just pierced Scrag to the heart."

"Don't I wish," said Jeremy.

Mall overhead music was loud when you were close to the ceiling speakers. Jeremy winced against the violins, jangling bells, and singers blasting by his ears, and flew through the giant baubles and wreathes dangling off the ceiling rather than going around them.

He watched Mom and Dana shop. Mom gripped Dana's hand as they made their way along the crowded walkways of the Mall of America. She also struggled with two heavy shopping bags. He could see that her nerves were frayed as she wove them through the streaming crowds. Dana's eyes, meanwhile, sparkled at the color and noise.

A tactfully roped off North Pole the size of an arena took up a main junction of the mall, covered with Styrofoam snow, a gingerbread-looking Santa's workshop, girls dressed as elves, animated reindeer figures, and Santa himself.

His cheeks needed no makeup to make them look rosy. His red suit, beard, and blanket of white hair looked hot enough to melt him. Still, he smiled and took child after child on his lap, or let the scared ones stand nearby, their faces hidden in Mom's knees, while hundreds of other kids and parents waited in line, some of the babies fussing.

Jeremy vowed never to be a Santa Claus. He flew closer to his family. "I'm too old for that," Dana announced, importantly, watching a little girl jabber to Santa. Mom spared a smile for her.

He knew what had Mom so edgy, and it made him so angry his pulse raced. Henry and Chuck sat on a Mall bench to the rear, sipping Orange Juliuses. She couldn't keep her eyes from drifting back to them. She'd probably seen them outside the apartment, too, constantly watching her and Dana. After Dad got on drugs before his arrest, she'd gotten good at spotting dangerous people.

Jeremy wanted to brain them, and the huge Christmas baubles right over their heads looked tempting, but he couldn't risk having them figure out he was here. He drew a huge breath to calm his temper.

Mom read the note again. He'd watched an older teen guy drop it on Mom's tray in the food court at lunch and earn a fast twenty bucks from Henry for it. She'd stared in terror at the slip of paper, then hastily shoved it in her pocket as Dana came bustling to the table with straws for their pop.

He hadn't had a chance to read it then, but he flitted directly over her now, determined to see it. "TALK TO A REPORTER OR THE POLICE AND WE'LL KILL YOUR KIDS," the note said in block letters. Jeremy stifled a groan of rage. They were wolves! Jackals! He couldn't believe he'd liked Henry, once upon a time.

"Mrs. Lapoint?"

The man's voice visibly startled her. She gripped Dana's shoulder, turning to glare.

Lee Englestad, the silver-haired newsperson from Channel 5, advanced on her. She would've hurried away from him if an older couple with a mall cart full of presents hadn't blocked her path. He stepped nearer. "Sorry to startle you, but, please. Stop avoiding me. Jeremy is above and beyond the other flying teens. I think that's why he wasn't filmed with the other students of the Higher Humanity Institute, and I think you know why."

Her voice shook. "I can't talk to you. I won't."

"The world needs the truth," he insisted.

She pushed on, clutching Dana's hand, forcing her to trot.

"Mom," she complained, "that hurts."

Jeremy stayed right with them. They made it across the intersection of two huge hallways. He hovered, looking back, surprised to see that Englestad stood in the same place, but with his head turned away from Mom and Dana. Jeremy followed his line of sight.

It couldn't be! He'd latched onto Henry and Chuck, still sitting on a distant bench, watching Mom scramble away from the reporter as if he were a werewolf.

But how would he know them? Jeremy thought hard ... Englestad had been at the HHI when Prouse made the big media announcement. Henry probably drove the shuttle van.

Englestad turned his face back toward Mom and Dana, and Jeremy saw fury in his eyes. He followed Mom and Dana, acting as their unofficial guard in an expensive coat. Jeremy's heart warmed to him.

They neared the mall center. Sounds of strong, good singing echoed off the walls. A crowd had gathered to hear a college choir singing carols, all dressed in red robes with white satin collars, standing on risers. There must have been a hundred voices lifted in harmony, no piano or other accompaniment needed.

Mom relaxed a little, gently touching Dana's shoulder. Dana watched the singers, drinking in each note, her face lit with a smile.

Jeremy caved in to what he wanted so badly to do. He flew over to one of smaller baubles hanging on the ceiling—only about the size of a soccer ball. He broke the clear plastic cord that held the bauble in place and flew directly over Henry with it. He and Chuck had sauntered after Mom and Dana, and now they sat again, taking the last open bench in the area and keeping an old woman from sitting. The lady looked tired. She turned away after searing them with a silent scolding they aptly ignored.

Meanwhile, the choir sang, "*Angels we have heard on high, sweetly singing o'er the plains. And the mountains in reply, echoing their joyous strains …*"

Jeremy dropped the bauble. It conked Henry's hands. His Orange Julius dumped in a gratifying splash all over his legs. He stood, swearing. The bauble bounced on the floor. The old lady whose seat they'd denied chuckled and clapped.

"Glo-o-o-o-ria!"

Chuck tried to help him clean it up but Henry shoved him away, ordering him loudly to, "Keep an eye on them." He spared one glance of fury at the ceiling. Jeremy waved at him.

Mom and Dana stayed put, listening to the choir. He wished they'd move on with Henry and Chuck so beautifully distracted. He hoped they'd lose them. If Prouse's bullies were going to make Mom so scared, they should at least have to work at it.

Jeremy watched Mom and Dana make their way across Level Three of the florescent-lit, open-air parking ramp, full of cold light and black shadows. Fright as icy as the wind showed in Mom's eyes.

They reached their rusted-out Toyota. She made sure it was empty, unlocked it, and all but threw the bags on the back seat.

She plopped onto the driver's seat, waiting feverishly to lock the doors the moment Dana got the passenger door pulled shut. But something made Dana gasp and stare at the seat, still standing, her eyes popping. She broke into a sudden smile, but Mom didn't notice.

"Get in the car," she ordered, sharp in her agitation. "What are you waiting for?"

She tried to ram the key in the ignition. Something blocked it.

"Mom, it's me," said Jeremy.

She caught hold of him, by feel, and hugged him hard, breaking into relieved tears.

"I'm fine," he assured her. "They don't know what I can do."

Jeremy stepped from an earthbound oval into Lee Englestad's office in the downtown Minneapolis headquarters building of Channel Five Television. The reporter, his hair a little less groomed for having just removed his hat, sat at his computer, studying a webpage. Jeremy drew near, impressed to see him studying a Bible research site. This page was devoted to the ancient Nephilim.

He made himself visible. "Mr. Englestad," he said gently, knowing the rise he'd get.

Englestad spun his office chair toward him, his eyes and body tense, and blurted out a swear word in his shock. He instantly apologized, introducing himself properly, his eyes gleaming with excitement.

"You're on the right track about us," said Jeremy, with a nod toward the webpage.

"Incredible!"

"The Nazis found the original Nephilim bodies and did something with them; made a formula or something. They injected the stuff into our grandparents, and that's how we got this way. The HHI students, I mean. See, we all had one grandparent that was in a German prison camp in World War II. I can't tell you any more, 'cause I can't read German."

"You found a report?"

"It's in Prouse's office. She's the HHI Director."

"I know. I was there when your classmates flew for the world. Why weren't you with them?"

"She's keeping me and two other boys locked in a room. We're the ones who found out about our grandparents. She doesn't know we can go through walls and other stuff."

"Clearly. And what you mean by 'other stuff,' I'd love to know. But about that report …"

"I'll try to get it to you. Promise me this, though, if I do get it, don't put it out there, like, to the public 'til I tell you. See, Prouse has these thug guys watching my Mom and little sister."

"I know," said Englestad, grimly. "I've seen them."

"I know you have. I watched you at the Mall of America. I was flying overhead, invisible." Jeremy couldn't resist throwing that in just to see the amazement in his eyes.

"I promise," said Englestad.

"I'll try and get it to you tonight."

"I'll be here. And be careful."

Jeremy turned, about to make a travel-way, but he stopped and faced him again. "Do you pray?"

Englestad was heading back to his computer. He paused, thoughtful.

"'Cause I think I'm gonna be in a big fight tonight."

Englestad frowned. "You shouldn't be fighting men like those two, no matter how amazing your new abilities are. They use guns and …"

"I won't be fighting men."

That took the breath clean out of the reporter. Jeremy let him draw his own conclusions. "I'll call my wife," he promised, when he could find his voice. "She's better at praying than I am."

"Does she have friends?" pressed Jeremy.

That drew a grin from Englestad. He nodded.

"I'm leaving now." Jeremy made an oval, unseen to Englestad, and stepped into it, disappearing instantly.

Englestad stood in shock. This kid came and went like a ghost. "You're not acting alone, are you?" he called out, in case he was still here. There was no answer, of course.

He sat down, rested his head on his hands for a moment to calm himself, and grabbed his cell phone. He speed-dialed his wife's number. While waiting, and with just a little shyness to it, he made the sign of the cross on himself.

Chapter 14

BATTLE

JEREMY, EPI, JOSH, and Tameeka passed into Prouse's bedroom to some of the loudest snoring that had ever rattled their ears. They stood there, snickering, to get it out of their systems. She was on her back, wearing flowery pajamas, her blankets up to her throat, buzzing like a motorcycle.

Dim moonlight shining through her half-open blinds showed them her neck was bare. So, where did she keep the file key while she slept? A quick look dashed their hopes that this would be easy. It wasn't on her dresser or the nightstand. Jeremy shielded his left hand with his right, made his little finger glow for a softer light, and passed his face and his left hand through the top of the stand.

He'd guessed right on the first try. It was in the stand's single drawer, still on its chain. He tested the drawer. Locked, of course.

However, this wasn't as intricate a lock as the one on the file drawer in her office. This one merely had a catch on a turning base, pointing up so that it stood against the inside of the dresser, holding the drawer closed.

It could be turned by hand. He worked at it, gingerly, setting his teeth against making noises that she could hear. It squeaked against the wood as his fingers fought to twist it down. The chainsaw snoring hiccupped and paused. Jeremy stayed dead still. Then Prouse gave a snort as loud as a pig's and continued rattling.

Jeremy pushed the catch down and opened the drawer.

The last obstacles between him and Report Number Twelve were the worst he'd ever imagined, and here he was, preparing to fight them. Epi, Josh, and Tameeka helped him do the old trick of shaping his bedding with rolled up blankets under it to make it look like he was sleeping, a string mop that Epi had swiped from a janitor's closet shaped like his head.

"It looks just like you," said Josh, grinning, watching Tameeka work the twisted mop strands into messy curls on Jeremy's pillow. "So cu-u-ute."

"Shut up," said Jeremy, without much heat behind it. He shot a spurt of lightning at the camera to wipe out what they'd been doing and moved to the corner, out of its view. He concentrated, his heart speeding up, and changed his clothing to his robe, the hem pulled between his legs and tied at his buckle, his weapons in place.

No more jokes now. "Can't believe you gonna fight those things," breathed Tameeka.

Epi formed a fist. "If I had a gun …"

"Bullets can't hurt demons," said Jeremy.

"That's the problem." Fright filled Epi's eyes and he poured out a stream of words as though a dam had broken. "Listen, can't you fight for our families, first? I got a letter from Mama today. Nobody knows where Sharp is. They seen the Man-Lady's thugs watching our house. Papa thinks Sharp did something to make a rival gang mad, and they're waiting around to kill him. My whole family is so scared!" His voice broke and he turned his back to them.

Jeremy stood helpless in his battle array. "Why didn't you say something earlier?"

"You were all busy with the plans, man. We gotta get the key. Gotta get the key."

Asiel chose that moment to appear. "Your troops await you," he announced.

Jeremy was suddenly torn when he should have been gearing up for his first-ever battle. Epi shot him a look over his shoulder and turned back, grimacing, looking mad at himself. "Sorry, man. I know you gotta do this thing. I'm being a coward."

"No, I'm scared for my family, too," said Jeremy, half-pleading. "But, I think we've gotta … trust God, here. We do what we're supposed to do and he'll take care of it."

"Well said," declared Asiel.

"I gotta go." Jeremy formed an oval.

"Good luck, hey," said Tameeka.

"Yeah, good luck," chimed in Josh.

Epi hastily wiped his eyes. "Hey, General Patton, fight good, okay?"

Jeremy saluted them and stepped into the travel-way.

He stood in the center of the alpine meadow in Glacier National Park, over fifty angels in a large circle around him, standing at alert attention, waiting on him. His heart hammered so hard he felt lightheaded. He drew in a huge breath and tried to stand taller. "You all know that I have to reach the file and get that report."

"We'll fend off the enemy," promised Asiel. "Though, you'll be busy enough, yourself."

"Yeah," he tried to say, except that his voice cut off. He shivered as if he'd been swimming in ice water. He breathed a prayer for help.

The warm, golden light grew around him, easing his quaking. He closed his eyes, murmuring thanks and worship. When he opened them again, seconds or maybe minutes later, he saw Asiel with his head bent. All the angels worshipped, the glow bathing the meadow.

The Hand was upon them. His body felt strong. His senses had grown so acute he could see a squirrel running up a tree fifty feet away and hear its claws click and clitter on the bark. He felt thrills of fear, not drowning waves. He was going to do this.

Jeremy pulled his sword from his scabbard, the blade ringing, the shining steel free of all gauzy protection now, the edges sharper than any earth-made razor. He hoisted it heavenward, one-armed, in strong salute. The others did the same.

"For truth!" he yelled.

"Truth!" roared the host.

"For the Lord of Hosts!"

"The Lord of Hosts!"

Jeremy shouldered his shield, made sure Prouse's file key hung securely on his neck, and formed an upright oval.

The three fat demon guards lolled around Prouse's office file. One sat on the cabinet. The lead guard stood in front, sharpening his claws with his twisted dagger.

Jeremy burst through the travel-way into Prouse's office shoulder-to-shoulder with Asiel, the other angels streaming in behind them. They were all so bright the demons could only snarl and turn their eyes away for the first moment of their appearing.

They also slammed their knobby shoulders together, their swords bristling at the ready. Jeremy set his teeth and charged, drawing back his sword like a batter waiting for the pitch. The lead guard met his attack, his teeth bared in a snarl.

Jeremy swung his sword. He struck the demon's iron blade and pushed it away. *Clang!* Now, back swing! *Clank!* Their blades hit again, sending a jarring shock up his arm. But he kept hold of his sword. He brought his shield to his hand, sliding it down his arm, grabbing the handgrip and bringing it up in moves he'd practiced until he could do them faster than thinking. He came back with a forehand stroke. The guard, hard pressed, fended it off with his spiky shield. *Clunk!* He growled, and it had a note of fear in it.

He was doing it! He was battling an opponent who found him a hard fighter. Elation soared in him, and he pressed the attack, his sword a blur, his shield fending off blow after blow. The lead guard could barely hold on.

One angel struck the right guard and another attacked the left. Their blades sang.

"Commander!" hollered the lead guard.

Scrag appeared. Asiel tore into him. Scrag met the onslaught with a riotous laugh and a shout: "Soldiers! To me-e-e-e!"

Demons by the dozens poured up from the floor, angels surging at them. Battle, that thing Jeremy had been so afraid of, was joined in full force. Now that he fought in the thick of it, parrying, thrusting, striking, and fending off hits with his shield, he felt little fear at all. He was too busy for it.

Englestad paced in front of his desk, talking excitedly on his cell phone. "Yeah, this is an enormous exclusive. I know it's risky. All we can do is wait on the kid."

His wall clock showed ten-forty-five P.M.

Spirit beings don't just fight on the ground. Jeremy caught fleeting images of angels and demons going at it in mid-air and on the ceiling—tumbling, leaping, and clashing like birds of prey, their wings flapping hard to keep them stable.

He danced about on the floor, busy enough. The lead guard bashed at his shield, hit after hit, and he backed up, letting his opponent think he was gaining the advantage.

He drew closer to the file with every step. Okay, close enough. He rapidly sheathed his sword and held his shield with both hands, preparing to leap.

"*Hah*-har!" gloated the lead guard. "The little boy angel is weak after all!"

That drew Scrag's eye. "Moron!" he roared, fending off a strike from Asiel. "You're letting the half-breed get to the file!"

Jeremy sprang in the air, snatching the key off his neck and raced for the drawer, top speed. Scrag made a power jump, blocking his way, mid-air, only two feet from the file. Jeremy did a wingover, dodging away before Scrag could catch him by the throat.

The guard had also taken to the air at Jeremy's heels. The kid spun away, and the guard found himself, unhappily, eye-to-eye with his commander. Scrag punched him so hard that he slammed against the outer wall, caught by surprise and unprepared to pass through it. He hit the floor with a thud.

"Useless worm, go wake her up!" Scrag hollered at him. The guard scrambled out through the wall.

Scrag hauled back his blade to kill Jeremy, frantically working to free his own sword. Asiel swooped between them and the duel that began in the HHI cafeteria raged again.

Jeremy hovered, gasping with relief that Asiel had intervened for him, as always. A demon that looked like a lizard with a hyena face grabbed his foot to jerk him to the floor. Jeremy walloped off its clawed hand. It shrieked and scuttled away.

A fat demon leaped to take its place as he landed. He met the thing's sword and cut its arm on the back swing. One of the guards joined against him. Two against one! He had to back up, his shield taking a pounding and his arm aching. His sword arm throbbed.

"Lightning," coached Asiel. How he had time to notice Jeremy's weakening arms in his own hot fight with Scrag, he'd never know. Dumb! How could he have forgotten? He aimed the point at the hyena-faced demon and sent a yellow ray at it. It seared under its shield and burned its hide. It tore away, shrieking.

Jeremy hit the guard with a beam. It covered its head and stumbled away.

He could take a second to breathe, but as he did, to his frustration he saw that he had been pushed half the room away from the file cabinet.

The lead guard appeared at Prouse's shoulder. She'd rolled to her side, snoring loudly. He rubbed his bruised ribs, cursing under his breath, and slapped her head. She gave a grunt. The snoring faded then rumbled on again.

Irked, the lead guard jumped on the bed, rocking it hard. She jerked awake, terrified by the moving bed but saw nothing. She sat up, staring at the mattress.

He rocked it again. She clutched the sides and cried out.

"Go to your office!" he barked in her ear.

She frowned, trying to shake off the disturbing thought.

"Office, stupid! Go!"

She stumbled out of bed and scuttled to her closet, grabbing slacks and a sweatshirt.

The battle, at its hottest, made a din that pounded against Jeremy's ears. The air crackled with lightning. Demons fell and the floor seemed to swallow them. Foul reinforcements rose to fill their ranks.

Angels also fell, sending pulsing sorrow through Jeremy, though he was too frantically busy to dwell on it. Their brother and sister angels hoisted their limp bodies into the arms of angels who soared down from the ceiling, then lifted them up to disappear through a heavenly stairway. He knew this: once he completed his job, the killing would end. He had to get to the file cabinet!

Out of the corner of his eye, as he fought two demons, he saw Asiel and Scrag, still battling in full fury. Nevertheless, he'd worked himself to within a yard of the cabinet, and Asiel kept Scrag too busy to see it.

A bear-sized creature with spiked fangs, standing guard at Scrag's orders, blocked the file. Jeremy zapped the two demons fighting him. They spun away. He sent a lightning blast at the bear-thing's legs. It hopped off, snarling.

He ran to the cabinet and jammed the key in the lock. They'd win the battle the moment he grabbed

Report Number Twelve and left through an earthly travel-way!

He turned the key, but before he could pull open the drawer, he felt an onrush and spun to meet it. The lead guard had returned, his black blade thrusting at Jeremy's shoulders. He brought up his shield, just in time. *Clunk!*

He had no choice but to fight him, trying to make the killing strike that would end the guard's attack and let him grab Report Number Twelve.

Too late. The door burst open and Prouse stormed in, hitting the lights, Mr. Bock at her heels. Jeremy thought their sudden entrance would end the battle, at once. It didn't. The invisible fight raged unchecked throughout the room as Prouse shut the door.

The two full-fledged humans blinked at what must be, to them, confusing flickers of light and shadow.

"Something's wrong with the lights," grumbled Prouse, glaring at the florescent overhead lamps. "Brat kid. Do you suppose he did something?"

Bock turned the lights off and on again. It didn't help. "Why blame Lapoint for the missing key? He's locked up."

"Don't count on it." She walked toward the file, slower than usual, her vision hampered by the erratic lighting. The bear-like demon, watching her, gave a throaty laugh and advanced on her, his dagger raised. Scrag pushed Asiel back and leaped to block her.

"Brainless! She's ours!" He kicked her attacker clear out through the wall, his squawks fading rapidly.

Prouse drew near the file.

Jeremy, in a panic, fended off a mighty swing from the lead guard. She'd see the key in the lock! He sprang in the air and lunged for it.

He reached the key a few yards ahead of Prouse and struggled to free it from the lock. The lead guard, furious at losing him, took to the air and dove through her, straight at Jeremy's back, his sword thrust forward.

Asiel gave a great shout. "Jeremy! Your back!"

Jeremy turned and hit the black sword away with his shield. Again he was so angry, he *z-z-zapped* the lead guard with such force he tumbled away, end over end. The flash of light stopped Prouse in her tracks.

The one second distraction for Asiel was all Scrag needed. He knocked Asiel's shield aside and struck. The iron blade sank deep into Asiel's chest. Scrag twisted and withdrew it, bellowing his triumph.

"Asie-e-e-l!" cried Jeremy.

Asiel fell backwards. Jeremy stood in shock, his sword and shield dangling. The lead guard leaped up and brandished his sword two-armed, to lop off his head.

Scrag hauled the guard back by the scruff. "He's not to die yet, and the credit will go to me."

He threw him out through the wall.

Asiel gasped in pain, his eyes clouding. Jeremy ran to him, fell to his knees, and grasped Asiel's hand. Other angels fought off the demons that would've jumped him.

Asiel's eyes closed. His ragged breathing stopped. His glow faded and went out.

Scrag shoved through them and brought his shield down on Jeremy's head. He fell facedown across Asiel's chest, out cold.

"Battle over-r-r!" bellowed Scrag, in triumph.

Chapter 15

THE WRATH OF PROUSE

ATALL ANGEL bore Asiel's body in his arms, flying slowly to a heavenly travel way. They disappeared. The few remaining angel soldiers dipped their heads in grief.

Two angels stood guard over Jeremy, lying on his back, still unconscious, his sword and shield at his sides, the file key still caught in his fist. "I wish we could take him with us," fretted one of them, a female.

"He's not allowed. He's still alive," answered her comrade. A soft, gold-colored glow formed around Jeremy. Scrag shielded his eyes, snarling. It was a fearsome glare to him, and it kept him and his cronies at bay. The last two angels rose and disappeared through a doorway to heaven.

Scrag and his three fat guards remained at the file.

⊣═⊱═⊢

To Prouse, the room lights settled down, at last, letting her see normally. She rifled through her desk, still looking for the key. She stalked to the file cabinet, on a thought, and tried the drawer. It opened.

"Unlocked!" she cried out, horrified. Her hand shot to Report Number Twelve. She pulled it out, relieved to see it intact. "But did he copy it?" she muttered.

"And how would he do that?" Bock demanded.

"I'm telling you, he's been out of that room."

"Let's check it then."

Mr. Bock would've left at once, however, his eyes landed on something in the middle of the floor. He stared, narrow-eyed, and moved closer, muttering in amazement. She also made out the small thing. It floated a few inches off the floor, a cord crimped around it.

"The file key," he blurted out. "On your neck chain. But …"

His foot touched something unseen that made him step back in haste. "What in the world?"

He knelt, his hands feeling along an object. His movements suggested an arm and a head. "It's a kid," he rattled. "Knocked out or something. Invisible!"

"Lapoint?"

"How should I know?"

Prouse snatched the chain and key from the unseen hand. "It is him."

She locked the drawer. "Get him to the room."

Mr. Bock was staring at her as if he couldn't believe that the strangeness of the situation wasn't affecting her. That made her all the angrier.

"Pick him up," she ordered him.

He lifted Jeremy, by feel, struggled to stand, and carried him, still out cold.

Scrag followed Prouse, Bock, and the half-breed; the guards understanding that if they left their post at the file, they'd wind up minus their wings.

Prouse threw open the door, holding it for Bock. Epi and Josh scrambled out of bed fully dressed. Bock came in looking odd, indeed. His arms seemed to be cradling something large, and he walked with the fast, stumbling steps of a man who bore a weight. But Epi could see nothing in his grasp.

Of course, neither he nor Josh were that dense. They could guess whom Bock held, and shared their dread in a look. Jeremy had surely lost his first spirit battle.

They kept their mouths shut and watched. Bock felt along Jeremy's unseen arm, muttering. "Elbow, here. Vein must be here."

Prouse pushed the medical cart in and brought it alongside him. Bock grabbed a blue rubber armband and tied it on Jeremy's right arm. It remained visible, suspended in mid-air in a squeezing circle. Jeremy moaned to the discomfort.

Epi and Josh went invisible by unspoken agreement.

Prouse, standing by the cart, noticed the room suddenly empty. "No!" she cried out. "You little … Mind the cart."

She blocked it on her side with her arms outspread. Bock did the same on his end. However, Epi and Josh had a huge advantage over them. They couldn't be seen; they were smaller by a lot; and they could take their time, looking for the best place to ease past them. It had to be like herding ghosts.

Epi tiptoed to Bock's end and ever so carefully worked his way in to stand between him and the cart, holding his breath. Several blood tubes and syringes lay in rows. If he could grab them away, Prouse couldn't use them against Jeremy. Josh had the same objective in mind, at the cart's other end, staring intently at the syringes.

Rrragh-h-h!" Scrag appeared in Josh's face! He yelped and cringed away.

Epi lunged for the blood tubes. He had time to snatch up four before Prouse saw them rising and made a grab. She knocked one from his hand. It clattered to the floor. He scrambled to kick it, still clutching three tubes.

Scrag caught his scruff and hauled him screaming off his feet. The demon threw him hard. Epi remembered, in a flash, that he could go through walls, or he would've slammed against it, breaking bones. He passed through. The vials didn't. He heard them clatter against the wall and bounce on the room floor, the sounds muffled, now that he was out of the room.

Josh hovered in the hallway, panting. "We gotta get back in there," said Epi, though the thought made him feel sick. Josh nodded. Shoulder to shoulder, they turned back and passed into the room.

Jeremy was groaning. His mattress moved. Prouse snatched up the blood tube at her feet and ran to him, uncapping the needle. She felt for his arm vein.

"Hold him down," she ordered Bock. He found Jeremy's shoulders and pinned them. Epi scuttled to Bock and kicked his ankle. He yelled and kicked out low, as though an invisible dog had just bit him.

Unfortunately, Epi quickly learned that no one was invisible to Scrag. The demon grabbed a fistful of his shirt and hefted him off the floor, growling in his face. Epi shrieked and struggled like a rabbit pulled from a trap. Scrag lost his hold on him. Josh tried to scuttle around the demon. Scrag blocked him and hauled back to kick him out of the room.

A cry of pain drew Epi's eyes to the bed. Prouse stabbed a needle into Jeremy's unseen arm. Bock clamped his hands on his shoulders, holding him down. Everyone in the room froze, watching the tube fill with dark burgundy fluid. Scrag laughed.

Prouse withdrew the needle and pressed gauze to the dot of blood that showed the pinhole in Jeremy's arm. Now it was her turn to laugh as she capped and pocketed the tube.

Then her laughter ended and her eyes turned as hard as agates. She reached for a clear, liquid-filled syringe. Scrag licked his lips.

Bock grimaced. "That will get us a death sentence. He's only a boy."

"He could destroy all we've worked our lifetime's for. This is for humanity."

Epi caught on in a rush of horror. He had no hope of flying around Scrag to save Jeremy. So he did the only possible thing. Scrag may be able to block them, grab them, throw them, and everything else physical, but he couldn't shut them up. "Jeremy!" shouted Epi, as loud as he could make it. "Get outta there! Don't let her stick you!"

Josh joined him in a jumble of racket. "It's poison! She's gonna kill you!"

"Fly! Fly! You gotta get away!"

"Jeremy!"

Prouse uncapped the needle.

In the hallway, their ears pressed to the door, Rachel and Tameeka heard the shouts. Tameeka, in a panic, raised her fists to pound the door with all her strength for a distraction.

Rachel grabbed her shoulders and shoved her away, blocking the door. Tameeka regained her balance, shocked. "What'd you do that for? Somethin' terrible is goin' on! Didn' you hear? Mrs. Prouse is going to …"

Rachel had hard fury in her eyes. "She's my grandma, and she's brilliant!"

Tameeka saw what she was up against and made up her mind in a millisecond. She vanished from Rachel's sight.

Rachel shrieked, staring in surprise at the place where Tameeka had been.

Jeremy woke up and went visible, still in his angel gown, a blinding white to Prouse's eyes. She hesitated only for a moment, and then grabbed his arm.

His friends kept up the yelling: "Don't let her stick you!"

"Fly, man!"

Jeremy barely had time to widen his eyes in fright before Prouse had jammed the needle in his vein and pushed the plunger.

Tameeka appeared, her hands to her mouth, moaning. He raised his eyes to her, startled by the sound, and then lowered them again, staring at the place where the needle had entered. He couldn't believe it had happened.

He drew a huge, panting breath. Tameeka stifled a sob. He looked to Prouse, standing stone still, holding the empty syringe upright … and went *nova bright!*

Tameeka yelled out in joy. Bock and Prouse cowered away. She dropped the empty syringe. It hit the floor and rolled. The poison had formed a huge wet spot on Jeremy's sheets, near the pillow, where the liquid had gone straight through him, harmlessly.

He yanked off the armband and rose in the air. "My weapons, please?" he asked Heaven quietly.

Three things happened at once: Scrag heard him and drew his sword, *zzhing!* Tameeka saw Scrag for the first time and *screamed!* Jeremy dove for the sword and shield that appeared on the bed. He landed and faced his enemy.

"I split your mighty angel's heart," Scrag taunted him. "I'll do the same to yours."

Jeremy set his teeth and struck. Their blades clashed, a blur of light and dark, the hammering of steel on iron filling the room.

The students and Mr. Bock watched, fascinated and frightened, as Jeremy battled something unseen. But Prouse would not be detracted. She grabbed another poison-filled syringe and felt around the room, unnoticed by the others.

Her fingers met Epi's back. She clutched his shirt, twisting it hard. Epi cried out and tried to writhe away. She uncapped the needle and grasped it like a dagger, to stab it in his back.

A shout as loud as a thunderclap came from the window. *"Perrillo!"*

Sharp appeared and dove toward her, catching her forearm, and twisting it. He wrenched the syringe from her hand, the needle jabbing the fleshy part of his thumb and sticking out the other side, no harm done. He hurled the syringe away. It smashed against the wall in a spray of poison.

Prouse threw punches at him. Sharp fended them off and drew back his fist to flatten her. Bock surged in and grabbed Sharp's arm. Sharp wrenched away from him. Prouse kicked at his knees. Bock grabbed him in a tackle hold.

Tameeka snatched a stack of hardcover books from the top shelf, flew over Bock, and dropped them. They thumped on his head and shoulders. He released Sharp and staggered back, covering his head. Epi grabbed his neck. Josh knocked his legs out from under him.

Bock thudded to the floor and lay gasping, the wind knocked out of him. Sharp had covered his head to keep from getting brained by books, too. He unwrapped his arms and set his tiger's eyes on Prouse.

It was time to retreat. She scuttled to the door, fumbling with the key. Sharp surged after her.

Jeremy gave a cry that drew all eyes. Scrag's blade had slashed his upper arm, slicing the gown. Blood ran down his arm, coating his hand.

Sharp glared hatred at Scrag.

"You can see the monster, too?" Epi asked his brother in amazement.

"Yeah."

Scrag laughed at that, even as he sprang for Jeremy. "I can appear to whoever I want," he boasted, pounding Jeremy's shield with his sword until it rang.

Jeremy was flagging. He clearly couldn't keep up the fight much longer.

Prouse pulled her cell phone from her pocket and hit speed dial. "Henry," she snapped. "Do it."

"No!" Jeremy cried. Prouse unlocked the door. Bock sprang to his feet and beat her to it, shoving it open and running down the hall.

Prouse followed in a hurry. Rachel still stood outside the door, looking confused. Her grandmother grabbed her arm and marched her with her.

"But Grandma," protested Rachel.

"Don't argue."

They disappeared around the corner to Prouse's office.

Jeremy gave Rachel one pained glance that she didn't even see. But he had no more time to waste. He made an earthly travel-way and hit Scrag away with a bolt, *bzzap*. Scrag staggered back. Jeremy shouldered his shield and dove for it. Scrag rebounded, catching him by the shield as fast as an alligator striking. He hauled Jeremy toward him, face to face, and what a terrible face, his breath hot and foul.

"Where do you think you're going?"

Jeremy shook off the shield strap. The shield dropped, clanging on the floor like a steel lid. He tried to kick free. "My family …"

"… is going to die." The demon raised his dagger to stab him. *Clunk!* Jeremy's shield slammed against Scrag's head. And again. Scrag lifted a shoulder against the hits and turned, snarling.

Epi held it by the side, hitting Scrag edge-on with all his strength. "Didn't expect that, did you, Ugly?" he said and smashed Scrag's head once again.

With a roar, Scrag threw Jeremy, who had the presence of mind to fly. He veered hard around, but his sword fell from his exhausted hand, ringing against the wood floor.

How much longer could he fight?

Scrag turned his fury on Epi who tried to hit him once more with the shield. The demon caught the edge and hurled it away as though it burned him. He raised his dagger and moved in for the kill.

Epi scuttled away, gasping, "Oh-h-h, Lord!"

Tameeka threw encyclopedias at Scrag. "Get a headache, Pig Face!" she yelled.

They passed through him, thudding harmlessly against the walls.

Sharp snatched up Jeremy's shield and threw it like a Frisbee. That worked. It was part of Scrag's realm. It crunched against his neck. He wheeled, growling. Sharp beat Jeremy to the downed sword and wielded it, bobbing on the balls of his feet.

"Come on, Ugly," he challenged the demon.

Laughing, Scrag unsheathed his sword.

Chapter 16

ALL FOR TRUTH

TWO GRAPPLING HOOKS, thrown together, clanged and caught on the wrought-iron railing of Jeremy's apartment balcony. The railings rocked and trembled to the weight of two men climbing. Chuck reached the top first and rolled over, his feet crunching in a fresh coat of snow. He hunkered down on his feet, like a baseball catcher. Henry climbed over and did the same.

Chuck hoisted a brick from the carpenter's pouches at his waist, rose up, and hurled it. It shattered the sliding door, thudded onto the kitchen floor, and rolled with the shards of glass it carried. He kicked in a larger hole and cautiously stepped through it. Henry followed. They were in. They drew handguns from their pockets.

Jeremy, in the worst panic of his life, watched someone else use his weapons. He needed them to save Mom and Dana. Yet, if he grabbed his sword and left, Scrag would kill Sharp … and Epi, Josh, and Tameeka, since they were part angel, too. What should he to do?

Sharp met Scrag's blade strike for strike like a born swordfighter. His fierce eyes shone and his feet danced. Scrag had to fight with all his being, the mocking grin turning to a grimace of anger.

But Sharp, untrained, could only fend off that black blade for so long. Scrag hit his sword with a twisting upper thrust and sent it spinning from his hands.

He didn't wait around for Scrag to run him through. He leaped in the air, flying fast. Scrag tensed for the spring and the chase.

Twang! Jeremy's bronze arrow pierced Scrag's elbow, pinning his arm to his side. Jeremy sent another. It sank into Scrag's neck. He roared, stumbling, and fell on his back with a thud that shook the room. Jeremy drew again, setting his mark on Scrag's chest.

"I'll kill you later, half-breed," Scrag vowed, and sank into the floor as Jeremy's arrow whacked into the boards where he had been.

Henry and Chuck stood in the living room doorway, black hulks in the dark. Chuck wasn't about to trip over a coffee table. He edged in, saw the square of a lamp stand, and clicked the lamp on low, showing the couch and easy chairs, Christmas decorations, and tinsel glistening dully on the tree.

They could hear movement in the room nearest to the living room. They heard the soft, quick steps that a nervous woman makes. Chuck walked quietly to the door and faced it, his handgun raised and ready to fire the moment she opened it.

Epi, Josh, and Tameeka cheered. Sharp grabbed up Jeremy's sword and handed it to him. Epi tossed him his shield.

He spun toward the travel-way, still shimmering in mid-air. "Hey, Zorro," called out Sharp, his urgency halting Jeremy. "You use that to get around?"

"You can see it? That's new. Yeah, I can go anywhere in a second. I don't know if you can. You could ask."

Sharp made the sign of the cross on himself, Epi doing the same almost in sync with him. "Hey, Lord God?" Sharp asked, gingerly. "Could I get to my family, like, right now? *Por favor?*"

A second oval appeared before him. Epi grabbed his arm. "Not without me."

Sharp and Epi disappeared into their travel-way. Jeremy stepped into his.

Josh found himself alone with Tameeka, and he wasn't a bit happy about it. She could only stare at the places where the ovals had been in pop-eyed astonishment.

"Tameeka!" he yelled. "Don't just stand there. Do you have a cell phone?"

That snapped her out of it. She pulled a pink flip phone from her pocket.

Jeremy burst into the front room of the apartment, blazing bright, his sword crackling, yelling with all his might. *"Ya-a-a-ah!"* He was so angry he felt hot enough to burn the building down.

Chuck brought the gun around, but the apparition shocked him into staring, frozen. Jeremy knocked the gun from his hand just as Mom stepped out in her nightgown and robe.

She shrieked.

Jeremy sent a single bolt of lightning at Chuck's shoulder. He clutched the burn and hollered, sprinting away, pounding through the kitchen.

"Now do you believe in angels?" Jeremy shouted after him. He heard a crash as Chuck broke the rest of the sliding door glass in his frenzy to escape.

Henry opened fire at him. *Crack! Crack!* The bullets passed through him and slammed into the wall a foot from Jeremy's mom. She shied away. Jeremy leaped in front of her, bringing up his shield for her sake, not his.

Henry fired again. The bullet pinged off the shield. Jeremy sent a bolt at him. He dodged it, running. He made for the door next to his mom's—It was Dana's room. He slammed it open and surged in.

Jeremy flew after him. "Leave her alone, Henry!"

He sent another bolt. Henry ducked. It missed him by inches. He reached the bed and hauled Dana out. She screamed, so high-pitched it was painful. Jeremy could send no more lightning or he'd hit her.

Henry wheeled, gripping her tightly, the gun at her throat. "I dunno what you think you are," he said, with surprising calmness, "but you drop that electric sword or I'll kill her."

Two men dressed in dark jackets and pants darted from shadow to shadow along the icy street of a cul-de-sac in Plymouth, Minnesota. This kind of neighborhood, with nice houses running down it and circling the round place at the end, shouldn't have had men like that sneaking around in it.

They made for Josh's house. Josh and Tameeka, invisible to all but each other, hovered over the intruders as they sneaked their way into the back.

"See?" whispered Tameeka. "I told you we needed to get here, like, right now. An' wasn't I right about the door or whatever that instant thing is? All you gotta do is ask."

"Yeah, yeah," said Josh, disgruntled. His head hurt from the astonishment and fright spinning around in him. Astonishment at finding himself all-of-a-sudden at home. Fright at the sight of men like that making for his house. "And you don't need to keep your voice down."

He saw car lights. A vehicle turned into the cul-de-sac. It had lights on its roof, too. Relief pulsed through him. Police! They'd taken his 9-1-1 call from Tameeka's cell phone seriously.

The car stopped in the circle. Cops jumped out, brandishing big flashlights.

Josh and Tameeka agreed to help the cops, no words needed. Josh flew over his roof. There! One of the thugs hid himself in the gap between the small, barn-shaped tool shed and the back fence. Josh soared over him and gave a fake sneeze. "Azzh-choo!"

Of course, the cops heard it. He wanted them to. The younger of the two officers dashed to the back yard, snow crunching under his feet. The thug bolted.

When it came to running on snow, Missouri men were no match for Minnesota cops. For one thing, they only wore tennis shoes, to the cops' winter boots with lots of grip. The officer had him down with cuffs on his wrists inside two minutes.

Josh soared to the front yard and watched the older, larger officer catch the other one with help from Tameeka. She landed and tripped the thug before he could reach the street. He made a magnificent stumble, his arms flailing. The cop made a Vikings' tackle and sent him facedown in the snow.

"Nice move, Tameeka," exulted Josh.

She was laughing. "Thanks!"

The officer was yelling at his catch. "Drop your weapon! Stay on the ground! On the ground!" He pulled the thug's arms behind his back and snapped on the cuffs. The thug whined something, his face buried in the white stuff.

"Oh, too bad if it's cold," said the officer. "Ya gotta dress warm in Minnesota."

Josh landed next to Tameeka. They clapped each other's hands like athletes who just won the game. Then just like that, they'd gone from antagonists to teammates.

The last two of Prouse's thugs sat in their car, parked in front of Epi and Sharp's house in East Los Angeles. Sharp and Epi suddenly appeared on the hood, incandescent, lighting the dark like a hundred streetlamps. Sharp smashed in the windshield with a crowbar he'd grabbed from Papa's garage, while the thugs wasted all their bullets shooting at them. They even danced a little, to prove bullets couldn't hurt them.

They flew off the hood. Sharp landed by the driver's side window and bashed it in. The driver peeled out like a drag racer. Sharp laughed as they disappeared down the street. Epi hovered, crowing.

Jeremy dropped his sword. Dana whimpered, her face as white as frost. Mom came to her door and stood rigid, her lips moving in frantic prayer.

What could he do? Henry had the upper hand.

A white-hot being flew down through an oval in the ceiling of Dana's room and landed a foot from Henry. It brandished a blazing sword and a golden shield and shouted with the strength of heaven, *"Ai-yah-h-h!"*

Jeremy knew that warm voice. Asiel!

Henry, terrorized, saw him. He took a one-armed hold on Dana's waist and fired one, two, three, four shots at the angel, the bangs as loud as bombs. Dana shrieked and covered her ears. Two shots glanced off Asiel's shield. The third and fourth zinged by Mom, out to the front room and hit the Christmas tree, shattering three ornaments.

Asiel raised his sword to strike. Henry held Dana like a shield, scuttled around the angel, and backed toward the bedroom door.

Jeremy waited in the hallway, eight feet off the floor. Mom stepped aside, her eyes locked on her daughter, as Henry cleared the doorway. Jeremy held his shield sidewise and up and down to his body, and glided silently over Henry. He slammed it down, edge-on into the man's face. *Thunk!* It crunched his nose and forehead, a divider between the gun and Dana. Henry grunted and tried to shove it away with his gun hand.

Jeremy held the shield firmly in place with one hand and with the other, wrenched the pistol from Henry's hand with fingers stronger than three men's. He sent the gun skittering down the hall so hard it raised sparks from the carpet.

He raised the shield and slammed it against Henry's head. The man sagged like a leaky sack. Jeremy hoisted Dana from his arms before she hit the floor. He didn't care in the least if Henry broke something.

Dana went from crying to laughing, and threw her arms around Jeremy's shoulders. He hugged her, hovering. Asiel strolled through her bedroom door, joining them in the front room. Jeremy dropped his shield and landed to give him a boisterous embrace, still holding Dana.

"I saw you die," Jeremy began, his eyes filming to the horrible memory and the joy he had now.

"The King of Heaven raised his son back to life and has done the same for his servant."

That made Jeremy laugh even as a tear or two fell. He hugged his brother angel once more.

Dana could see Asiel. Her eyes shone, and she giggled to find herself squeezed between them. Jeremy set her down. Mom knelt and grabbed her, sobbing her relief.

Dana patted her back, but her eyes stayed on Asiel. "Hello, Angel," she said.

"Hello, Dana. Mrs. Lapoint." Asiel bowed to both. Jeremy lifted Mom to her feet. She stared at Asiel, unable to get a word out. Then she pulled her mind to business, crushing her son in a hug.

He could barely get enough air to talk. "Hey, Asiel," he gasped out. "I thought angels couldn't hurt humans. You wouldn't really have done anything to Henry, would you?"

Asiel shrugged lightly. "No. But a man like that doesn't know the rules."

Jeremy grinned. The crazy wails of sirens came to their ears, growing louder. He saw pulsing red and blue light reflecting off the snow on the balcony.

"Mrs. Junge called the police," said Mom, her voice quavering.

They heard feet pounding up the hall stairs and then solid knocking and a strong woman's voice. "*Police*. Open the door."

"Mom, I gotta go," said Jeremy. "I've gotta get hold of something important."

She glared at the dried blood on his arm. "No, but you're hurt … !"

He kissed her face and Dana's, ignoring her. Asiel made an oval.

Dana kept her eyes locked on her brother until they disappeared.

Chapter 17

TRUE CHRISTMAS

JEREMY STEPPED INTO Prouse's office, his sword bared, tense and ready.

Relief! No fat demon guards stood around the file. But that gave rise to a hateful question that tightened his chest once more. *Why not?*

He tore to the black file cabinet, Asiel quietly at his back. No! The top drawer was unlocked. He pulled it open. A huge gap stood in the midst of the row of upright files. He gave a cry of helpless anger. Report Number Twelve was gone.

"We're too late!"

"I feared we may be," said Asiel, "with no guards left here."

"I promised Mr. Englestad. I blew it!"

"You saved your family, as you were meant to."

That did a little to neutralize his acid anger, but he was confused. "Wasn't I meant to get the report? Then why did we fight?"

"All things work together," said Asiel, briskly. "Come! Prouse may still be here."

That spurred Jeremy into action. Speeding on the hunt, he and Asiel zoomed out of room, shoulder-to-shoulder and invisible to the rest of the world.

Louisa Prouse raced along the two-lane highway, her Cadillac floored, doing ninety-five miles per hour.

Bock gripped the dashboard. His seatbelt, as tight as a straight jacket, kept him from slamming into the door or worse, into her on this curvy road.

"You could draw a patrolman, driving this crazy," he whined.

As if in answer, flaring red and blue lights appeared ahead, and they heard the pulse of sirens, rising in pitch as they drew near.

Prouse pulled her foot from the gas. They slowed down rapidly. She hit the brakes and made a harsh swerve to the gravel shoulder, the dutiful driver clearing the road for police on an emergency run. The Cadillac jounced to a stop.

Two patrol cars screamed by them. They quickly vanished from sight and sound, cut off by the curves and woods of the Missouri road.

Prouse continued, laughing, keeping her speed to a sensible sixty. An "Interstate 70" shield sign showed an arrow under it pointing to the right. They reached the entrance ramp. Prouse accelerated to freeway speed and freedom.

Report Number Twelve was stowed in her locked briefcase, securely wedged between the driver's seat and the back seat, right behind her.

Jeremy flew slowly out of Walker Hall, disappointment weighing him almost to the ground. The Man-Lady and Mr. Wimpy Bock had escaped, and Report Number Twelve was gone with them. If only he'd gotten back to Prouse's office in time!

He spotted the other HHI students, wearing jackets, huddled outside Fletcher Dorm, staring at the whirling lights of cop cars as officers strode in and out of Walker Hall. He soared over to them and landed near his friends, keeping himself invisible to all of them. He wanted to know what was going on, but he was in no mood for conversation.

Mona trotted over to the group. "You all gotta get back inside. The police need to question you."

Melissa spoke up for them, as a matter of course. "For what? What's happened?"

"The school's gotta close."

They reacted with a babble of protests and questions. Melissa made herself heard over it all. "Where's Mrs. Prouse?"

Mona held up a quieting hand. "Mrs. Prouse and Mr. Bock left in her car in a big ol' hurry. I dunno why they did. The cops wanna find 'em, though."

She walked away, and the teens took up angry muttering.

Sharp, Epi, Josh, and Tameeka stood off to the side, in the deep shadows of the building. "Who called the cops?" asked Sharp. "You, Bergren?"

Josh shook his head.

"I did," declared Tameeka. "I figured they'd believe a girl better than a boy."

The boys snorted. "So, where's Jeremy?" asked Epi. "Ain't he made it back, yet? Do you think Henry coulda got him?"

Jeremy appeared in front of him and five inches from his face. "With what? Bullets?"

Epi yelped and hopped back. "You're gonna kill me the way you do that."

They asked eager questions, all at once. Jeremy rode over them. "Where's Rachel?"

"Her parents just got here," Tameeka told him. "The police are askin' her questions."

"Why? She didn't do anything wrong."

Tameeka winced. "I'm sorry, this is gonna hurt, but she and I overheard the Man-Lady tryin' to kill you. I was gonna pound on the door, but Rachel pushed me away from it."

"No way!" It was a cry of pain, and it drew Melissa to him like an angry mom descending on some unlucky coach. "Why are the cops here, Lapoint? And why did Mrs. Prouse have to leave so fast? Because of you?"

Tameeka turned on her like a spitting cat. "Mrs. Prouse tried to kill Jeremy! She knew what we are, Jeremy was gonna prove it, and she tried to inject him with poison. He been tellin' us the truth all along. Do you hear me? We are *part angel!*"

For once, Melissa was rendered speechless.

Rachel stepped out of Walker Hall flanked by her parents. She paused, having heard Tameeka. The entire campus heard her.

Jeremy made a move toward her, desperate to talk to her. She dropped her eyes and hurried on, her mother glaring at him as if he were a rabid dog. They reached their car and drove off, and he could only watch helplessly.

Epi broke the uncomfortable silence. "Those investigators, they got the syringes with the poison in them. I went and watched them. They searched every inch of the jail room and put everything on that cart in bags. They got the ones off the floor and the empty one by the bed, too. And the bed sheet with the poison on it. Smoking gun, man."

"I just looked in the lab," said Josh. "The Man-Lady and Bock took a lot of lab stuff away. There's hardly anything left in there except the animals. No blood vials in the freezer, either."

"What do they want our blood for?" asked Tameeka.

Sharp spoke up as matter-of-fact as if he told them they were having oatmeal for breakfast. "To make more of us."

That shocked even Tameeka into silence. She recovered and kept up her dogged questions. "But Report Number Twelve that you fought for ... you got it, right?"

Jeremy kicked a rock. "I got back too late."

"Then how we gonna prove that we part angel?" Tameeka wasn't asking the question so much as voicing her disappointment. She could join the club, as far as that went.

But a fire began in Jeremy, flaring rapidly. He turned to the rest of the student body, clustered a little beyond his closest friends, and raised his voice in a challenge.

"Do any of the rest of you believe we're Nephilim?"

They looked at him in silence.

"Well, if you do, join us."

More silence. Then Carl surprised them all by stepping out and walking over to Jeremy to stand by him. Tameeka grinned at him.

Nine others quietly joined Carl.

"We'll show the world," said Jeremy, his eyes afire.

Melissa folded her arms and stayed back with the rest.

Three days later, the stained glass windows of the Basilica of St. Mary glinted in the bright-but-cold sunlight of a late December afternoon in downtown Minneapolis. The church was enormous, all in stone, gracefully carved, majestic and immovable. It was a Twin Cities' landmark.

The city had roped off the parking lot. Thousands of people in coats, caps, and gloves milled about in it, jammed almost shoulder to shoulder. Many of them waved jubilant signs: "ANGELS ARE REAL!" and "GLORY TO GOD IN THE HIGHEST!" The crowd whistled, cheered, yelled, and did everything else it could to make a joyful noise.

Jeremy waited in the Basilica foyer, as hyper as the twelve other young Nephilim clustered around him. Their high-pitched voices and giggles echoed off the walls.

Lee Englestad stepped in front of them, quieting them in an instant. "You realize this won't change the minds of those who don't want to believe?"

"So what?" answered Jeremy. "It'll strengthen those who do."

The others agreed in murmurs.

"You're all very wise for you age," said Englestad.

"I'm not giving up on getting Report Number Twelve, either," Jeremy promised him. It still rankled him that he'd had to appear empty-handed in Englestad's office at one o'clock in the morning the night the HHI closed. "I'm going to keep looking for it."

"What d'you mean, you are?" demanded Tameeka. "We are."

That surprised Jeremy, but he'd learned, by now, that what Tameeka decided, she did. And to his amazement, the others looked every bit as determined to help him.

"But you've all got school, too, and …"

Tameeka cut him off crisply. "Spring break. Summer vacation. Weekends."

And that was that. Jeremy felt warmed through. These were the best friends he'd ever had. The only ones he'd had in while, come to think of it. "Mr. Englestad, you're gonna get your exclusive on Report Number Twelve."

"I'm counting on it," said Englestad. "And there are more ways than one of proving you've got the genes of the Nephilim in you. Genetic researchers at the University of Minnesota want to study you."

"Oh, good," moaned Epi. "More blood samples."

"What about Rachel Prouse?" asked Tameeka. "None of her grandparents were prisoners of the Nazis."

Jeremy, frowning, voiced what he had been mulling over for a week. "You know what I think it means? Dr. Praus injected his own daughter, Louisa, with Nephilim serum when she was a little girl. She didn't get the traits because they stayed dormant in our grandparents, skipped our parents, and flared in us. In Rachel."

"That's too gruesome," said Tameeka.

Englestad interrupted the discussion. "Interesting, but now's not the time, people. You've got a show to do."

They switched modes at once to hyperactive and hopping-nervous.

He opened the Basilica's front door. Cheers erupted. Englestad's camera operator had his video cam ready on his shoulder. He filmed the teens trotting to form three lines on the church's front steps.

Other news crews jostled each other to get what footage they could.

Marcy, Dana, Grandma Jean and Grandpa Leonard, Josh's parents, and grandma, Tameeka's mom and grandparents, and Epi's Mom, Dad, Grandpa, and little brothers and sisters stood in the front row of spectators. So did the core families of the other young Nephilim. Aunts, uncles, cousins, and friends crowded in behind them. And alongside them all, quietly refusing to join his fellow HHI students, stood Sharp, aloof and mysterious. Would he ever be anything else?

The camera operator focused on Englestad, standing to the side of the teen formation. He raised his voice. "Here they are, ladies and gentlemen. So, how 'bout it, young people? Are you part angel?"

On that cue, they took off and formed a line in the air, Jeremy at the center, rock music blaring from giant speakers around the lot. People shrieked, clapped, and whistled. They went luminescent. People screamed.

They'd practiced this for hours. At Jeremy's cue, they broke the line apart to spin, loop, and zigzag. One at a time, they flew clean through the steeple to yells and shrieks redoubled.

Then they caught hands, formed a "V" with Jeremy at the apex, and did a giant loop. They ended the show with a low, fast swoop over the audience to wild applause.

Prison guards stood at the doors of the TV lounge. An artificial Christmas tree with no lights on it and silk-wrapped, plastic ornaments on its branches took up the room's back corner.

Folding chairs bolted to floor runners sat in rows. Two dozen prisoners dressed in baggy orange tunics and pants watched the Five O'clock News on Channel Five. Mark Lapoint, lanky and blond, with his son's piercing blue eyes and blond hair, sat front-row-center, wrapped up in what he saw. The others, even the guards, had amazement in their eyes.

On screen, Jeremy and company, as bright as neon kids, finished their above-the-crowd loop and flew straight over the camera, the rock music thumping.

The prisoners erupted in cheering. Men clapped Mark's back. He sat in a daze. Even the guards grinned.

On Christmas Eve evening, Jeremy carefully stepped from an earthly travel-way into his father's prison cell, staying invisible until he got his bearings.

Dad's little digital clock on his lamp stand read 9:47. The flip calendar showed November 22nd. Dad hadn't cared enough to keep it up to the correct day. A photo in a plastic frame sat by the clock. It showed Mom, Jeremy at nine years old, and Dana at five.

Dad sat on his bed with his head bowed, looking so sad it put a lump in Jeremy's throat that felt like a tennis ball.

He swallowed it away. The hallway beyond the cell bars stood cold and empty. Jeremy took hold of all his courage and made himself visible to one person only.

He knew he'd startle him. He couldn't do anything about it. He spoke out, ever so softly. "Dad?"

Mark leaped to his feet, his eyes bugging out. But he had the presence of mind to whisper. "Jeremy! What the—? How the—? You shouldn't be here."

He ran to the bars and scanned the hallway. "If they see you …"

Jeremy had no need to whisper, but he kept his voice down so Dad would match his volume. "Dad, it's okay. The only one who can see and hear me is you."

Mark spun to face him, his eyes wild.

"It's part of the angel thing." Jeremy chuckled tightly, awkwardness getting the better of him. "Didja see me on TV?" he couldn't help asking.

Mark swallowed, visibly fighting to calm down. "Well, yeah. I mean … My kid!"

That made them both laugh a little, as stiff as boards. Jeremy's words spilled out fast. "I'm here 'cause it's Christmas, and I didn't want to not see you and 'cause we got you, Mom, Dana and me …"

He opted to show, not tell. He pulled a small, lidded box with a flattened bow on it from his pocket. The travel-ways let things of this realm pass through them.

He held it toward Dad, who took it slowly, and removed the lid. A man's watch rested on white gauze inside it. He took it out and slipped it on his wrist.

"Nice. Real nice," he mumbled.

"Merry Christmas, Dad," said Jeremy, his voice catching.

That did it. They broke into tears. Mark surged to his son and grabbed him in a crushing hug that Jeremy returned with much the same strength.

Opened gifts sat in clusters amidst mangled boxes. The tree, which had been stacked to the branches with presents, now stood empty underneath. Any cousin under ten years old played with their new toys. The rest of the family watched the Ten O'clock News on Grandma and Grandpa's big screen TV. Mom and Dana stood together against the back wall, waiting for something.

Jeremy stepped out of an earthly oval into the darkened hallway and made his way into the room, quietly. Mom and Dana rushed to him with eager whispers, asking about Dad. Was he okay? How did he look? Did he like the watch? He answered their questions while Mom wiped away her tears and hugged him hard.

He felt warm from his heart out. Dana wanted a closer look at his new iPod. He pulled it from his pocket. It was the latest model, in metallic red, and it could hold more songs than he could listen to in a year, once he downloaded them. And that warmed him all the more. Mom had kept a Christmas card addressed to him from Mr. Lee Englestad for the last present he'd open tonight. It had held a gift certificate for fifty dollars worth of song downloads. Englestad had schemed with Mom, of course.

The rest of the family, meanwhile, was reacting with oohs and ahs at something on television. Jeremy looked and saw himself flying. Oh, yeah. Channel Five News at Ten. They were repeating the St. Mary's Basilica footage in honor of Christmas.

Mom's sisters noticed the three of them standing and shooed kids off the curved couch, urging them to sit. They made their way to the place of honor. Grandpa, meanwhile, turned off the TV. He stood in front of his family, holding a large, well-worn Bible. The kids quieted down to shushes from every female over fifteen.

Grandpa gave Jeremy a shiny look. "Our grandson," he murmured, to chuckles. He wiped his nose on his cloth handkerchief and stuffed it away again in his back pocket (grossing Jeremy out).

He opened the Bible, cleared his throat, and read. "And there were shepherds living out in the field nearby, keeping watch over their flocks at night. An angel of the Lord appeared to them, and the glory of the Lord shone around them, and they were terrified …"

Jeremy imagined the scene. He saw shepherds wearing heavy robes, for warmth, some of them girded at the loins. They sat on rocks, quietly talking or stood near the dark, humped shapes of sleeping sheep. They had rods at their belts and staffs in their hands.

Suddenly the sky filled with a mass of light too bright, at first, to let them see anything else. They cried out and turned away. The sheep woke up and bleated, some of them wanting to run. And fright or no fright, the men and boys had to settle them down, taking stands around the flock, hemming them in, keeping most of them from bolting. A few took off. Men lunged after them, catching them around the

217

chests with the crooks of their staffs and pulling them back to their sides.

The shepherds kept their backs to the light, too scared to look, though the very ground glowed around them. Then the light seemed to gentle down, though it was still so vivid they could almost hear it.

Or was it distant voices they heard?

"Do not be afraid." The speaker had a rich, masculine voice that drew their eyes. The High Angel Gabriel stood before them, tall and strong, his golden-red hair gleaming and his eyes shining like sun on the water. "I bring you good tidings of great joy that will be for all people. Today in the town of David a Savior has been born to you; he is Christ the Lord."

And as Grandpa read, Jeremy went, in his mind, to the inside of a cave on the outskirts of Bethlehem, warm with the body heat of cattle and donkeys resting on their tethers, the scent and rustle of hay in the air. The light was very dim from a single sconce candle set firmly in a wall clamp, well away from the dried grass.

Mary lay in a mound of it, recovering, her eyes closed, her breath still ragged, sweat standing out on her forehead. Her husband was too busy to give her comfort yet. He cleaned the newborn in his arms with a wad of linen, checked to make certain his mouth and nose were clear, and wrapped him in a clean cloth from his shoulders to his feet.

Joseph carried him to Mary and slid his free arm about her shoulders, helping her sit up and lean in to him. She took her son in her arms, she and Joseph beaming. The baby grunted and sneezed, struggling to draw his first big breath. She caressed his face.

He coughed and let out one little, trembling complaint, then opened his mouth and cried with gusto.

"Suddenly a great company of the heavenly host appeared with the angel," read Grandpa, "praising God and saying, 'Glory to God in the highest, and on earth peace to men on whom his favor rests.'"

And Jeremy's mind went back to the shepherds' hillside. There, in the midst of the angels gathered in the sky around Gabriel, he saw Asiel. And a little behind him he saw Barzel. They sang "Gloria" in woven lines of melody and harmony that echoed off the hillside and pulsed all the way to the stars. Jeremy's spirit joined in the singing.

Grandpa closed the Bible. The rest of the family rose from their places and meandered to the snack counter where Grandma set out plates of cookies, crackers, and lunchmeat. The aunts brought out Thermos bottles of hot apple cider and coffee. The kids played again. The adults chatted warmly.

Jeremy didn't notice a thing around him. Dana, who had taken to watching him a lot, saw him wrapped in a soft golden glow.

Kathryn Dahlstrom 32156 Highway 47 NW
Cambridge, MN 55008
763-957-0997
kathryn.dahlstrom@yahoo.com

Represented by:
Mr. Leslie H. Stobbe
Literary Agent
300 Doubleday Road
Tryon, NC 28782
(828) 859-5964
lhstobbe123@gmail.com